A special note
of interest to the reader

Harlequin Books were first published in 1949. The original book was entitled "The Manatee" and was identified as Book No. 1 — since then over seventeen hundred titles have been published, each numbered in sequence.

As readers are introduced to Harlequin Romances, very often they wish to obtain older titles. In the main, these books are sought by number, rather than necessarily by title or author.

To supply this demand, Harlequin prints an assortment of "old" titles every year, and these are made available to all bookselling stores via special Harlequin Jamboree displays.

As these books are exact reprints of the original Harlequin Romances, you may indeed find a few typographical errors, etc., because we apparently were not as careful in our younger days as we are now. None the less, we hope you enjoy this "old" reprint, and we apologize for any errors you may find.

SPRING COMES TO HARLEY STREET

WELCOME

TO THE WONDERFUL WORLD

of Harlequin Romances!

Interesting, informative and entertaining,
each Harlequin Romance portrays an appealing
love story. Harlequin Romances take you
to faraway places — places with real people
facing real love situations — and
you become part of their story.

As publishers of Harlequin Romances, we're extremely
proud of our books (we've been publishing
them since 1954). We're proud also that Harlequin
Romances are North America's most-read
paperback romances.

Eight new titles are released every month and are
sold at nearly all book-selling stores across
Canada and the United States.

A free catalogue listing all available Harlequin Romances
can be yours by writing to the

HARLEQUIN READER SERVICE,
M.P.O. Box 707, Niagara Falls, N.Y. 14302.
Canadian address: Stratford, Ontario, Canada.

or use order coupon at back of book.

We sincerely hope you enjoy reading
this Harlequin Romance.

Yours truly,

THE PUBLISHERS
Harlequin Romances

SPRING COMES TO HARLEY STREET

by

DOROTHY RIVERS

Original Harlequin edition published
under the title "Harley Street Surgeon"

HARLEQUIN BOOKS

TORONTO
WINNIPEG

Original hard cover edition published in 1957
by Mills & Boon Limited.

© Dorothy Rivers 1957

Harlequin edition published January 1961 under
the title "Harley Street Surgeon" (No. 567)

Reprinted 1961

This Harlequin edition printed 1974

Printed in Canada

CHAPTER ONE

THERE WERE three bells by the door. By each of them a neat brass label gleamed in the autumn sunshine.

"Davenport. Private," said the top label.

"Dr. J. E. K. Gairloch," said the middle one.

"Mr. Barclay Davenport," said the label for the ground-floor bell.

Verity Cator went up the shallow steps, hesitated for a moment while she read the labels, pressed the lowest bell, and waited, outwardly composed and cool, inwardly tense. Behind her cars and taxis, and pedestrians as preoccupied as herself, went along Harley Street about their business.

The door was opened by a plump dark girl of about her own age, which was twenty-five, wearing a crisp white overall. Verity said, "I've come from Miss Monroe's Employment Agency about the vacant post."

"Oh, yes! They telephoned. We were expecting you. Please come in." She led the way across a hall whose carpets felt as deep and soft as moss beneath one's feet, into a large quiet room. "If you'll wait here, I will find out if Mr. Davenport is ready to see you."

Verity wondered why it was the surgeon she must see for this preliminary interview, rather than his mother, who would be her employer if she got the post. She never wanted to have dealings with another man as long as she lived. . . . But beggars can't be choosers, she reflected wryly.

She looked about her. She was in a lofty room whose two tall windows looked out into Harley Street. The plum-colored carpet fitted closely to the panelled walls. Long curtains of green damask matched the upholstery of the deep chairs and sofa. An electric fire resembling burning logs took the faint nip out of the October afternoon. On a long refectory table lay the daily papers and the latest periodicals, and on a smaller table stood a great vase of carnations, white and rose and crimson, spicing the air with their clove-scented sweetness. Evidently the removal of appendixes and tonsils and what-have-you must be a highly remunerative occupation—at any rate, in such a neighborhood as this!

She hoped she wouldn't be kept waiting long. It would be a relief when the suspense was over, and she knew her fate. Taking up the *Telegraph*, Verity perched on the edge of an armchair and began to study the "Situations Vacant" columns. But though her eyes were focused on the paper, her worried mind refused to concentrate on what she read. She put the paper down, opened her black calf handbag, and counted what was left of her money. Two pounds at least she owed to the hostel where she had spent the three nights she had been in London. There remained one pound note, three half-crowns, a shilling and some coppers between herself and—what? She didn't know. She couldn't imagine what happened to you when your life was pulled up by the roots, and there was no one you could turn to, and you had no money left and couldn't find work. The people at the employment agency had been noncommittal, but it had been obvious that they were not optimistic about finding her a post, after she had confessed her lack of any qualifications. Yet for such a post as this, surely she had been qualified by past experience!

In a flash, her thoughts had leaped the miles, and Verity was far away in Norfolk, in the past she was determined to forget. She was back once more at Bleydon, known to all the village as "the big house," for though it wasn't really very large, it was the biggest there. She saw again the long white windows looking out across the lawn towards the cliff top, whence a path zigzagged perilously downward to the beach. She heard the murmur of the sea, mingling with the sighing of the ilex trees behind the house. She laid away the linen on shelves that smelt of cedar, perched on the kitchen table while with Hannah, the old cook who had presided there as long as she remembered, she discusssed some new dish that might tempt her aunt's capricious appetite. She wandered in the old walled garden, gay with all the flowers of spring, sat there with the invalid in some sunny, sheltered corner where she had pushed Aunt Laura in her wheelchair, there to read aloud to her, or make her laugh with bits of local gossip gleaned on a shopping expedition to the village.

She had never realized how sheltered life had been. Yet, looking back, it seemed the sun had always shone at Bleydon until two years ago the stormclouds had begun to gather. To Aunt Laura's physical ill health there had been added mental failing, swift and tragic. Verity had suffered the distress of seeing her sweet temper turning sour and irritable, her gentle nature growing suspicious and morose, her kind and generous heart becoming bitter and vindictive.

The day had come when Dr. Lacky told her, "Verity, my dear, this is something you can't handle any longer on your own. Experience is needed now, for your aunt's sake as well as yours. We've got to get a nurse.

And so Nurse Kilsallow had come to take charge: plump and dark and thirty-five-ish, with big brown eyes that always slid away from yours to look beyond you, and a beguiling Irish brogue.

Fragments of talk echoed in Verity's mind. Dr. Lacky saying uneasily, "There's something I don't entirely care for about Nurse Kilsallow. Can't put a finger on it, but somehow I wouldn't trust her very far."

Her own voice, answering, "I feel like that about her, too."

"Would you like me to see if I can get hold of someone else?"

"Oh, no, no! I have no reason for disliking her. It's just a silly feeling. She keeps Aunt Laura happy, and that's really all that matters. And besides, what harm can she do?"

She heard again that creamy Irish voice, telling her, "I think Miss Cator's best left to herself this morning. She had a poor night." . . . "Miss Cator doesn't want to be disturbed." . . . "Miss Cator doesn't want you to read to her today. She'd rather be alone, she says." . . . "I think it would be wiser if you didn't take your aunt out in her chair this afternoon. She's tired. It might be too much for her. I left her dozing off into a nice nap. Why don't you take your chance of going off to have some fun with your friends?"

So Verity, believing her, had gone off to play tennis with Anne Lacky and her brother Alan, back from Oxford, and Euan Gilmerton, home on leave from Aldershot. She had been much surprised, when she returned to Bleydon, to be told by Hannah that she had been barely out of sight when after all Nurse Kilsallow had wheeled out Miss Cator in her chair!

Now, looking back, she marvelled that she could have been so gullible, so blind to what was going on. How could she have been so unaware of the wedge so quietly, so guilefully being driven between herself and her only living relative, who had been like a mother to her since her own mother died when she could barely walk! Perhaps she might not have been so obtuse to what was happening, if all her being had not been engrossed in her first and only love affair, with Euan Gilmerton. She could hear his voice now, telling her that he adored her. She could see his handsome fair head bent to hers, his teasing blue eyes looking in her own, could feel the hard strength of his arm, holding her close, his mouth, so ardent and demanding, on her own. . . .

Euan was in the Guards, the only son of a retired Major-General who with his wife had come a few months earlier to settle in a small house in the village. They had been very nice to Verity, and had seemed delighted with the news that she and Euan were engaged: news that would be kept secret until next time he came on leave, since for the present Miss Cator was not well enough to be told of it. But her condition grew no better, and a week before Euan was due back in Norfolk, Aunt Laura had died suddenly in her sleep.

Verity was about to telephone to the old family lawyer, Mr. Ketteridge, when a stranger had arrived, bringing the will, dated only six weeks earlier. He had given Verity a copy. Now she knew the reason for the look of secret triumph she had thought she must have been imagining in the Irish nurse's sly brown eyes of late, for everything that Laura Cator had possessed was left to Deirdre Maureen Kilsallow. Verity was not mentioned.

Euan had telephoned that night from Aldershot, his words conventionally sympathetic, his voice full of suppressed excitement. "My poor sweet, it must be simply grim for you! I've told my C.O., how the land lies, and he's letting me start my leave a week before it's due, so I'll be with you by midday tomorrow. Look, it's a bit soon to talk of plans, but I've been wondering if you'd like me to give up the Army? You'd hate leaving Bleydon, and anyway I'm sick of soldiering. I could soon find something to fill in the time. I might stand for the County Council. We could take a bit of shooting. . . . Think it over, darling, and we can discuss it when I see you."

Verity had told him what had happened, sure of his sympathy, certain he would understand how she was feeling over having to leave the house that had been home as long as she remembered. She had expected him to say they must be married quietly at once. But the distant voice had sounded angry and aghast and far from sympathetic as Euan cried that it was monstrous—she must fight the will—plead mental incapacity and undue influence. "Your lawyer will know the line to take. You'd better get him on to it at once. That nurse won't have a leg to stand on, if you go to law!"

"I've had a talk with Mr. Ketteridge. He says just as you do, that I ought to fight it. But I won't! Aunt Laura brought me up and educated me and never grudged a penny that she spent on me. She——"

"She got an unpaid housekeeper companion, let me remind you!"

"That simply doesn't enter into it. How could it? She was like a mother to me. I can't bear to think that towards the end, in her poor muddled mind, she must have felt that I'd abandoned her. That hurts far more than anything. Far more than leaving Bleydon. And I should feel still worse about it if I were to fight her will. It would be so disgustingly ungrateful if I were to fight her last wish."

Euan had argued with her, but in vain. In vain, too, she had waited for the one thing that could comfort her in this desolate hour—Euan's decision that they must marry

11

as soon as it could be arranged. Instead, he had said stiffly, "This makes the situation between us extremely difficult. I mean, I've nothing but my pay, you know. . . ."

So the last ruins of her world came crashing down. For a moment the shock of it had stunned her, silencing her while the pips sounded for the third time. Then, mercifully, pride came to the rescue of her anguished heart, and even put a note of amused mockery in her voice as she replied, "Poor Euan! You got yourself engaged to someone you believed to be the heiress to a handsome income and a pleasant house — and now you find she's nothing of the kind. Highly embarrassing for you! But don't worry. Our engagement's at an end. Good-bye!"

She had replaced the receiver without listening to his stammered protestations. That was the last that she had heard of him.

She had left Bleydon early on the morning after her aunt's funeral. Friends in the neighborhood had been kind. By telephone and letter she had had many invitations to stay until her plans were settled, but her one longing was to get away as soon as possible from everything and everyone she knew, and start a new life where there would be nothing to remind her of the past. So she had told no one of her plans, and had said goodbye to nobody save kind old Hannah, who was going to share her sister's cottage in the village.

Verity had told herself that she would never trust another man, that she had done with love for ever. The wheels of the train bearing her to London chanted in her ears with brisk finality, "Never again—never again—never again—" Yet, while her mind held only scorn for Euan, still her heart was filled with longing for him. Love, strangely mingled with contempt and loathing, still survived her struggle to extinguish it.

And here she was, three days later, sick at heart and disillusioned and alone, with twenty-eight-and-ninepence in her bag between herself and destitution. She'd simply *got* to get this post. She must—she *must*!

The girl who had admitted her returned. "Mr. Davenport will see you now. Will you come this way?"

She led the way across the hall, opened a door, announced "Miss Cator" and stood aside for Verity to enter. A girl in a dark dress, carrying a pad and pencil, reminded her employer in a discreet manner that Lady Bannatyne's appointment was in twenty minutes and withdrew, closing the door noiselessly behind her.

The room was walled with bookshelves. Since it was at the back of the house, the roar of traffic here was muted to a soothing murmur. From behind an outsize desk rose a tall man, powerfully built, and younger than Verity had expected. She had pictured the successful surgeon as a man of fifty at the least. He looked no more than thirty-five.

Courteous but unsmiling, Mr. Davenport said, "Good afternoon, Miss Cator. Will you sit here?"

Obediently she took the chair he indicated, aware that it was placed deliberately where the light from the long window must fall fully on her face, the better for him to take stock of her.

Later, trying to sum up that first impression of Barclay Davenport, Verity remembered black hair growing crisply on a shapely head, and above all a general effect of squareness: square brow, square, determined chin, straight, square-tipped nose whose nostrils, lightly flared, gave indication of an impatient temperament. But for the moment her attention was concentrated on the cool grey eyes regarding her inscrutably from beneath dark brows. He looked, she thought, as though he knew exactly what he wanted out of life, and would not rest until he had it.

Barclay Davenport betrayed no sign of his exasperation as he looked at her. Having pictured in his mind, and described over the telephone to the agency, someone in the early forties, capable and kind and cosy and experienced, it was infuriating to find himself confronted by a slender chit of a girl who looked no more than twenty-two or thereabouts! The physician in him noted automatically how she gripped her hands together in her lap, betraying tension that was undesirable: he wanted to get hold of someone tranquil and serene. The male in him was conscious that although she wasn't pretty, she was none the less remarkably attractive. Her nose was too short, but her teeth were white and even. Her grey eyes looked too large for her thin face, but they were luminous, their lashes long and silky. And her mouth, although it was too large for beauty, was disturbing. And because of these things, added to her youth, the prospective employer decided that she wouldn't do. The people at the agency had been mad to send her! Still, since she was here, he must go through the farce of interviewing her.

He said abruptly, "You look very young!"

Defensively she answered, "Twenty-five."

"I told the agency I must have someone at least ten years older. However, since you're here, I had better tell you my requirements.—I live in this house, in a flat on the top floor. My mother lives with me. For some time she has been more or less an invalid. Because of the condition of her heart, it is essential for her to be shielded from the slightest strain of worry or responsibility. That, by the way, is why she isn't interviewing you herself. Until two days ago, a cousin lived with us. She ran the flat, and kept my mother company. Unfortunately, on Tuesday she had to leave us at a moment's notice, owing to an emergency in her more immediate family. It looks as though she won't be able to return to us. In consequence, I must find someone suitable to take her place, as soon as possible."

Verity said, "Could you give me some idea of what I'd have to do, if I—if you were to engage me?"

Controlling his impatience at this waste of time, he said, "Your first consideration would have to be my mother's comfort and well-being. You would have to change her library books, arrange the flowers for her, try to prevent her from overdoing things. And you would run the flat. We have a morning housemaid who does all that's necessary in the way of cleaning, and a cook who comes in daily too, but you would have to order meals, and do the shopping, and so on."

"It doesn't sound too difficult."

"Perhaps not. Frankly, though, I'm afraid you are too young and inexperineced to take it on. For one thing, Mrs. Bream, the cook, like many good cooks, is temperamental. Handling her requires, at times, considerable tact. I understand you've never had a post of any kind before?"

"No. But I have experience of managing a house and staff. For the last seven years, since I left school, I've kept house for an aunt in Norfolk. She was an invalid, so I had entire responsibility for everything. We had a cook and daily help. A gardener, too. And latterly a nurse."

M'm. That certainly did sound more promising than he'd expected. If only she had been a few years older... !

As he considered pros and cons, Verity could sense his doubts, although his keen grey eyes were enigmatic. Her pride, still raw from her experience with Euan, rebelled. She would have given a great deal to tell this darkly domineering man that the post was not what she wanted, and bid him an aloof "Good afternoon!" But with no more than twenty-eight-and-ninepence in her bag, pride was a luxury beyond her means.

She said, "I would consider coming for a month, on trial. Then, if it didn't work, you would have time meanwhile to look for someone you considered suitable."

Though Barclay Davenport had little hope that anyone so young could take the place that had been filled so satisfactorily by his middle-aged cousin, he realized that to discover the ideal substitute would be by no means easy. And if she didn't fill the bill, at least this plan of hers that she should come on a month's trial would give him time to look around for somebody who did.

So, five minutes later, Verity was in a taxi, on the way to fetch her luggage from the hostel.

CHAPTER TWO

ON THE LAST morning of October, Verity let herself into the house in Harley Street, not without difficulty, since one arm clasped a sheaf of rose and rosy-mauve chrysanthemums, and from her other hand hung several heavy parcels.

The lift was at the top floor. Burdened as she was, she did not feel inclined to climb two flights of stairs. She pressed the button, and stood there, waiting.

Glancing at the closed door of the consulting-room she wondered whether Barclay Davenport were there, and if so, what scene was being played out a few yards from where she stood. Was that calm, crisp voice of his even now quietly questioning some patient, while his skilled hands probed the secrets hidden by shrinking flesh and muscle? Were his keen eyes noting symptoms that, invisible to the layman, to him revealed the answer to a riddle whose solution he was seeking? . . . Would it distress him if he had to give a tragic verdict? Or rejoice him if he could end the torture of suspense by a reassuring sentence?

Although she had been here for three weeks, she knew no more of his enigmatic personality than at their first encounter. One reason was that she had seen very little of him. After breakfasting alone, he left the flat and seldom reappeared much before six o'clock, when it was his habit, seldom broken, to spend an hour or so with Mrs. Davenport. Often he dined out with friends. Most of last week he had been at The Hague, attending some congress taking place there. So she had had little chance of learning anything about him at first hand. It was from Mary Pridham, the receptionist, Ellen the morning housemaid, while they made the beds, and his mother, over tea beside the fire, that she had gleaned the little that she knew. It seemed that having neither wealth nor influence behind him, it

16

was the combination of ambition, hard work, a forceful personality, and his natural brilliance as a surgeon that had brought Barclay Davenport in record time from the obscurity of a small town in the provinces to his present eminence. He must be kind, for Ellen never tired of telling her of how, on hearing of her sister's baffling illness, he had made all arrangements for her to be under observation in St. Machael's, and had himself performed the operation that had saved her life. He had a sense of humor; often she had heard his laugh ring out when he was with Mrs. Davenport.

Had he, before arriving in the Mecca of his profession— Harley Street—been quite as arrogant, as self-assured, as now? While Verity was speculating, the lift sank down and stopped, and simultaneously the door of the consulting-room opened. Barclay Davenport came out, glanced at her laden hands, and in two strides was beside her. As he slid back the door, his dark sleeve brushed her cheek. Faintly an odor of some disinfectant mingled with that of shaving soap.

"Will you tell my mother Dr. Gairloch is back, and will be having dinner with us this evening?" he said.

"I'll tell her at once."

As the lift bore her upward, Verity was irritated that her mind should linger on the memory of his hand, closing the door behind her—broad palm, long, strong, sensitive fingers. She didn't want to think of him—or any other man.

She switched her thought to speculating about Dr. Gairloch, who tenanted the first floor. She was a woman psychiatrist who for the last month had been in America on a lecture tour. Verity knew no more of her than that Mary Pridham, the receptionist, disliked her. Idly she wondered why . . . It mightn't be a bad idea to suggest to Mary that they should go together to a film tonight. The Davenports would probably appreciate her absence when they had a guest, and the receptionist was glad to have her company on a mid-week outing, as she lived alone in "digs" and went home to her family in Hampshire at the week-ends. The two girls had gone to several films together.

Verity took her parcels to the kitchen. From the beginning she had been careful to disarm possible hostility towards herself on the part of the temperamental cook by making it quite clear that, far from being a dictatorial new broom, she regarded herself and Mrs. Bream as friendly partners in the running of the household. Now, as she entered the bright little white-and-yellow kitchen, the broad red face that looked up from the greasing of a pudding basin wore a welcoming expression.

"Did ye think to bring the lemons for ma pancakes?" Mrs. Bream demanded, in the cosy accent she had brought with her from Galashiels some thirty years ago.

"Yes. And I've brought the groceries you wanted, too, to be on the safe side. I know Bramswell and Harris sometimes don't deliver till the afternoon."

"That was real thoughtful of you! I can be getting on now with the cleaning of the fruit to make ma Christmas puddings." Her approval was reward for Verity's sore fingers, stinging where the string had grooved them.

"There will be a guest for dinner," she told the cook. "Dr. Gairloch is coming up."

"Her! So she's back, is she?" Mrs. Bream sniffed expressively. It sounded as though she, too, disliked the doctor on the first floor. "The beef olives won't do the four of you."

"I may go to a film. I can have something out."

"What—fling away good money when you only have to say and you can have an omelet any time you fancy? The idea!"

Verity laughed and thanked her. Going in search of Mrs. Davenport, she found her in the spacious sitting-room, restful in cream and green and rosy-lilac. Mrs. Davenport was writing letters at her bureau, between the two tall windows. No one would have suspected from the appearance of the elegant woman with the satiny white hair, bright dark eyes, and lively expression, that she was an invalid. Yet several times during the past three weeks Verity had seen her lie back suddenly in her chair or on her pillows, blindly groping for the tiny heart-shaped box of Battersea enamel that held the pills for these emergencies: pills which mercifully acted magically quick-

18

ly, to the relief not only of the sufferer, but of the girl who watched her anxiously, wishing she could help.

There was no sign about her now of illness as she looked up, smiling. "What glorious colors! Perfect for this room. How clever of you!" Gently she touched a crisply curling petal. "In spring I'm always certain that my favorite flowers are freesias. Later on, I'm quite convinced they're roses. But now I know that they're chrysanthemums! How I love that bitter autumn scent of theirs!"

Verity smiled back at her affectionately. Having dreaded that she might be a fretful and exacting invalid, and as imperious as her domineering son, she had been captivated at their first encounter by the older woman's friendliness and charm. Her outlook was so young, her smile so gay. She was so understanding and considerate, had such a keen, quick sense of humor.

She said, "I met Dr. Davenport in the hall on my way in. He asked me to tell you Dr. Gairloch is back, and he has asked her to dinner this evening. I thought, if you don't need me, I might go to a film."

"Just as you like. There's no need to absent yourself because we have a guest. Still—Janice Gairloch does love talking shop with Barry, and you might find it tedious. I know I do! If it gets too much for me I shall escape by saying I'm tired, and go to bed."

So, when she had done the flowers, Verity got in touch with Mary Pridham on the house telephone, and they arranged to go together to a film that evening.

The afternoon passed much as usual. When she had settled Mrs. Davenport on the *chaise longue* in her room, to rest till tea time, Verity changed the library books, then went for a walk, past Marshall and Snelgrove's, across Oxford Street, down Bond Street, along Piccadilly, and back by way of Regent Street.

Now and then some woman's elegance made her feel acutely conscious of her own shabbiness. After Nurse Kilsallow had come to Bleydon, Aunt Laura, formerly so generous to the girl who had been more like a daughter to her than a niece, had taken to doling out a pound or so at long and longer intervals, instead of giving her the regular allowance she had had since leaving school. Gradually Verity's wardrobe had reached such a low ebb that there had been very little fit to bring away with her Longingly she gazed in the shop windows. She had no wish for a mink coat nor a glamorous evening gown, but now and then she paused, while her eyes lingered wistfully on a well-cut suit or tailored frock. She looked a long time at a coat in glowing garnet red, luxuriously collared in beaver, ruefully aware of her own shabby tweed, that had seen hard service for the last three years. How lovely it would be, when at last she could afford a new one! But for the present, though her salary was generous, she must save every penny that she could, lest when her probation ended a week hence she found herself once more homeless and unemployed.

She longed to know her fate. She wouldn't have believed, if anyone had told her three short weeks ago, that she could so speedily take root in unfamiliar surroundings a-mong strangers; still less that she could so soon recover from the agony of disillusion over Euan. Her pride still stung when she thought of him, but her heart felt nothing. Nothing at all! And having found that love could die so easily, Verity had decided that it obviously wasn't worth either the having or the giving. Well—at least she'd learnt her lesson. Love should have no part in her life from now on. She would take good care to guard both heart and pride from further anguish on that score! Friendship and work one liked—with these, life surely could be full and happy. All in good time she would find friends. And mean-while, work she liked was hers . . . if only she could keep it. . . .

Back in Harley Street, she found the lift again at the top floor. This time, since she was not burdened with a load of heavy groceries, rather than wait for it she began to climb the stairs. As she reached the top of the first flight, Dr. Gairloch's door opened. A woman came out, so that they were face to face. The stranger's air of being on her own ground made it evident that this was neither visitor nor patient, but Dr. Gairloch herself.

Almost without knowing it, during the last week or two Verity had gradually built up a mental picture of the absent tenant of the first floor. She had imagined her as being a short, brisk woman nearing sixty, always clad in grey, mannishly tailored; a woman who scorned the use of make-up on her clever face, whose short grey hair was sleek as pewter, and brushed back like a man's; whose gimlet eyes would sum one up dispassionately through hornrimmed spectacles, a woman who had little interest in anything save her career.

The reality was so different from her imagining that her eyes widened in surprise. The woman who confronted her could be little more than thirty. She had the fair, pale coloring, very faintly tinged with green, that one associates with water nymphs. Straight greenish-gold hair was swept back from her high brow like a silken cap into a big knot on her neck. Her eyes were green as the edge of a glass shelf. Even her matt skin had a greenish pallor, untouched by any make-up, though she had used light brown mascara on her lashes, and rose-pink lipstick on the mobile, thin-lipped mouth between a long nose, sharp at the tip, and pointed chin. As though she wished deliberately to accentuate her curious greenish coloring, she wore a suit of heavy roughish silk in the soft, pale, grey-green of willows. She was no beauty, yet many a pretty woman might have envied her distinction, her arresting air of elegance, the poise and magnetism that would make heads turn in her direction in any company. This, thought Verity, must be what people meant when they spoke of a *"belle laide."*

"I am Dr. Gairloch. What can I do for you?"

Verity realized that by standing rooted to the leafgreen carpet, instead of going on her way, she had given the impression that her destination was the first floor. She felt her face flush as she stammered, "Thank you— I'm on my way to the top floor—I work there. . . ."

The cool green eyes changed from indifference to appraisal. Verity suddenly acutely conscious of the shiny places on her suede shoes, the worn cuffs of her coat.

"I suppose you've taken Ellen's place? I didn't know that she was leaving."

"Ellen is still here, but Miss Duncan—Mrs. Davenport's cousin—had to leave rather suddenly to see to family affairs."

"How very unfortunate!"

A rejoinder seemed unnecessary, so Verity went on her way. Climbing the second flight of stairs, she wondered if she had imagined the expression of hostility in those pale appraising eyes? Surely one couldn't feel acute dislike for anyone after an exchange of barely half a dozen sentences? Or could one? Was it perhaps a case of "Dr. Fell"?

She felt a curious chill of apprehension and foreboding. But it's ridiculous to feel like this! she told herself. It's most unlikely we shall ever meet, except occasionally on the stairs or in the hall. And anyway, she can't do anything to harm me, even if she wanted to—which is highly improbable!

None the less, a feeling of uneasiness returned from time to time to haunt her while she had tea by the fire with Mrs. Davenport, ate the omelet Mrs. Bream prepared an hour before the normal time for dinner, and set off to meet Mary Pridham, until finally the tumbling seas and screaming gales of *Moby Dick* banished it from her mind.

It was nearly eleven that night when Verity returned to Harley Street. The tall house was uncannily quiet; she felt as if it were alive, resenting her intrusion, as she crept up quietly to the top floor.

Tiptoeing to the door of Mrs. Davenport's bedroom, she paused to listen for any sound of movement from within; if she were wakeful about this time, a hot drink often lulled her to a good night's rest. As she stood there with straining ears, she heard her own name spoken in the drawing-room a few yards away. The door was not quite closed, and every word spoken in Dr. Gairloch's cool, carrying voice came to her clearly.

"—this Cator girl is obviously not at all the right type. *Poor* Mrs. Davenport! Too bad that Miss Duncan had to leave while I was abroad— I would have gladly found her someone suitable."

Of Barclay Davenport's deep-toned rejoinder Verity caught only three words: "—but my mother——"

"My dear Barclay, naturally your mother wouldn't tell you how she feels about the girl! The very last thing she would want would be to bother you. But the poor dear must long, in her secluded life, for the companionship of someone of her own kind."

"Of her own kind—" as though I were a—a Hottentot! thought the listener, furiously.

Dr. Gairloch went on, "Luckily I know of someone who is exactly what she wants. A Miss Blackett. Forty-ish, capable and experienced and cultured."

"D'you mean to tell me," said the deep voice drily, "such a treasure isn't cherished by some doting employer?"

"She has been with old lady Rousse, in Mount Street. But I see in today's *Times* that Lady Rousse is dead. Leave it to me! I'll telephone to Miss Blackett first thing in the morning and find out when she can come. It would be worth your while to give the Cator girl a month's salary in lieu of wages, to get your mother happily settled."

In her preoccupation Verity had been unconscious that her handbag had been gradually sliding from beneath her arm. Now, as Barclay Davenport was saying, "That's extremely good of you. I——" the bag fell with a muffled thud. She swooped upon it. As she rose, the drawing-room door was flung wide, and she found herself confronting Barclay Davenport.

Disjointedly she said, "I'm sorry for disturbing you—I dropped my bag—I meant to creep in quietly for fear of waking Mrs. Davenport, if she has gone to bed. . . "

"My mother went to bed an hour ago. She wasn't feeling very grand. I gave her an injection, and she must be sound asleep now. Good night!"

"Good night."

Her lips were dry, her throat felt parched. She longed to have a cup of hot sweet tea, but, longing still more to be shut away in her own room, she passed the invitation of the open kitchen door, thankfully closed her bedroom door behind her, and sank on to a chair, gripping her hands together on her lap, so tightly that the knuckles were white.

A conflict of emotions tore her. She was bewildered and incredulous that their brief encounter had made Dr. Gairloch her enemy, furiously angry that the doctor should be trying to do her harm behind her back, desperately afraid of what might come of her malicious interference. Why, why should a woman who had so much— security, a home, success in her profession—seek to harm a girl with none

23

of these things, a countrified nonentity who couldn't vie with her in any way, who scarcely came within her orbit?

Presently she took off her coat and dress, hung them away, put on her dressing gown, and automatically began to brush her hair. Suddenly another aspect of the situation struck her: humiliating memory of being discovered by Barclay Davenport, listening to a conversation not intended for her ears. Eavesdropping, to put it bluntly! What must he think of her?

It was the last straw. She flung herself upon the bed and wept, sobbing like a small unhappy child, until she was jerked back to self-control by a brisk knock on her door. Her first thought was that Mrs. Davenport was ill, and needed her. Forgetting all else, she sprang up and opened the door, only remembering her dishevelment and tear stains when she found herself face to face with Barclay Davenport. Luckily her back was to the light. Perhaps he wouldn't notice that her eyes were red and swollen.

Imperturbably he said, "I'm sorry to disturb you at this hour, but I must have a word with you. I shan't have time to spare tomorrow morning. I'll be waiting for you by the fire." The words were no request, but a command. He closed the door, not waiting for assent.

What now? Did Dr. Gairloch have so much influence with him that he couldn't rest until he'd told her she must leave as soon as possible? Would Mrs. Davenport have no say in the matter?

As she splashed cold water on her face, and combed her tangled hair, Verity found small comfort in deciding that at least she'd give herself the satisfaction of explaining that her eavesdropping had been accidental.

CHAPTER THREE

VERITY FOUND Barclay Davenport standing waiting for her by the fire. He took one glance at her, then went to a tray of drinks on a small table in the corner, and began pouring something into a glass.

She couldn't wait. She said, her eyes fixed on his broad, flat shoulders, "Mr. Davenport, I——" Her voice was husky. She cleared her throat, and tried again. "Mr. Davenport, I'd hate you to believe I was deliberately listening to your conversation with Dr. Gairloch. I didn't even know that she was still here, when I came in. I was being as quiet as I could, afraid of disturbing Mrs. Davenport. Outside her door I stopped to listen, wondering if she were awake—and then I heard my name—and after that I listened automatically, not quite realizing what I was doing. I hadn't been there more than a few moments when you found me. I felt simply *awful!* I do hope you understand!"

He came towards her. "My dear girl, you explained all that before. Of course I understand!" He handed her the glass he carried. "Drink this."

Obediently she gulped a mouthful, making a wry face.

"Why have you been crying your eyes out?" he asked her. "Not about that, surely?"

His eyes were keen and searching. She avoided meeting them. "Oh—a variety of things!" she answered, looking at the fire. "What did you want to say to me?"

"That can wait. I want to get this sorted out first. How much did you hear of what was said?"

"Does it really matter?" she evaded him.

"Yes. You may have got a false impression."

"I gathered Dr. Gairloch considers me 'the wrong type' to be here, and wants you to get someone else as soon as possible. Someone she considers suitable."

"And did you also 'gather' my reactions?"

25

"No. Your voice is not so penetrating."

"I told her it was no concern of hers or mine. The decision is my mother's. And before she left, I told her that I personally consider you to be entirely what my mother needs. A square peg in a square hole. D'you like being here? D'you want to stay?"

Relief had for the moment lowered the guard of her reserve against him. Looking up, she met his eyes and found them kind and understanding. Her own were shining with relief and hope. "Oh, *yes*!"

"Good!—finish your drink. You're looking better for it."

Obediently she sipped again. Noting her grimace, he said half ruefully, half in amusement, "Too bad that you don't appreciate the best Napoleon brandy! Next time you need reviving, I shall search the kitchen for the stuff that's used in brandy butter!"

He took her empty glass. "That's that. Now for the other matter. I brought you here at this unreasonable hour because I'm troubled about my mother. As you know, she had a rather nasty 'turn' soon after dinner. She must have a day or two in bed. She's pretty certain to protest— she hates to feel she's giving in. But as I must start operating at St. Michael's first thing in the morning, and she may sleep late after the injection I gave her, I shan't be here myself to take a firm line with her. Will you tell her it's an order? And that I have arranged for Dr. Anderson to see her during the morning?"

"Certainly I will. How worrying! Is there any special reason why she should be worse?"

"She was agitated by a cable from my sister in Rhodesia. Oh, not bad news—Jill and her husband and their little girl are coming home on leave next month, a good six months before we were expecting them. My mother was overjoyed, of course, but the excitement was too much for her."

"I'll see to it that she keeps very quiet tomorrow," Verity assured him as she went back to her room with lightened heart.

She lay awake for sometime, going over in her mind the happenings of the evening; dwelling first on the unpleas-

26

ant episode of Dr. Gairloch's attempt to oust her, then forgetting it in speculation about the travellers from Rhodesia. Often Mrs. Davenport had talked about her only daughter, as they sat together by the fire, Verity mending linen while the older woman added tiny stitches to an evening bag of petit point that she was making Jill for Christmas. It was three years since she had seen her daughter and John Staverley, her son-in-law; Julia their small daughter, had been only nine months old the last time they left England for Rhodesia, where John was a mining engineer. Mrs. Davenport adored them, all three. Under the glass top of her petticoated dressing table were arranged numerous photographs and snapshots of the trio: Jill, a dark-haired girl with smiling, candid eyes, her pleasant-looking fair young husband, and a large-eyed solemn baby girl at various stages, ranging from a tiny infant lying on a rug to her present age of nearly four. What change, if any, would their coming make to her own prospects of remaining here? The one spare bedroom was no more than large enough for two. Would her own room be needed for the little girl? Would Mrs. Davenport want the presence of an outsider, when her own daughter would be here to bear her company?

Her thoughts turned back to Barclay Davenport. When for a few minutes he had lowered his façade of aloof inscrutability, she had glimpsed a side of him she had not hitherto suspected, humor and kindliness and—yes, and charm. One could imagine that to some women he must be irresistibly attractive. And there must, of course, be women in his life, women with whom as like as not he spent his evenings when he did not dine at home, superbly groomed, fresh from the hairdresser and the beauty parlor, gay and alluring and provocative. . . .

Next morning Mrs. Davenport, happily excited over last night's good news, seemed quite content to stay in bed. When Verity came to take away her breakfast tray she plunged at once into making plans for the homecoming.

"As soon as we know the exact date of their arrival, we shall book one of those service flats in Cavendish Square. In one way it's a pity that there isn't room to have them here, but there they will be near us, and at the same time independent."

Verity breathed a sigh of thankfulness that after all her room would not be needed for them.

"It's wonderful to think that they'll be here for Christmas! Julia is at just the most enchanting age, when it will all be sheer magic to her. That reminds me, Verity—what about your own plans for it? You know we'd love you to stay here and join in all our family doings. But if you'd rather go away for a few days, spend it with relatives or friends, of course we'd understand."

"Then—does that mean you want me to stay on here permanently?"

"My dear, of course! Didn't you realize that? How stupid of me! You fit in so perfectly that I took it quite for granted you would know I wanted you to stay."

The sudden ending of anxiety was so poignant that it was an effort to concentrate on what Mrs. Davenport was saying now.

"—so now that's happily settled, let's get back to Christmas plans. No hurry to decide. Make up your mind at leisure what you'd like to do."

The Lackys would be glad to have me, Verity reflected. Or the Somers. Or the Reids. Or almost anyone at Bleydon. But I can't go back there! I can't face the pity. And above all, I can't run the risk of meeting Euan, or his people. . . .

"I would like to spend it here, with you," she said. Mrs. Davenport was evidently delighted, though she added, "But I'm sorry you have no one of your own to go to, none the less. You must feel very lonely, sometimes?"

Now that she was going to stay on here permanently, it would be good manners to tell Mrs. Davenport something of her life and background. This seemed as good an opening as any other. Haltingly she said, "Just before I came here I went through rather an unhappy time. I'd like to tell you, if it wouldn't bore you?"

"Far from it!" Mrs. Davenport assured her. She had sensed a mystery often, wondering why it was that an attractive girl of twenty-five seemed to have neither family nor friends, and neither wrote a letter nor received any.

So Verity told her sympathetic listener of her life at Bleydon with her aunt, of the coming of Nurse Kilsallow and all it had entailed, of her love affair with Euan, followed by the bitterness of disillusion when on Aunt Laura's death it had transpired he had not loved her for herself, but as the heiress he had taken her to be. It was surprising how the telling cleared away the last remaining shreds of ugliness that lingered in her mind, turning a fresh page for the writing of the future.

That evening Barclay, drinking a glass of sherry in his mother's room before dinner, remarked, "You must have had a dull day, I'm afraid."

"Not at all! I always enjoy a visit from Dr. Anderson, he's so entertaining in his pawky way. And Verity has been telling me her story." Then, since Verity, not thinking that it was a story of sufficient interest to be worth repeating, had not said that it was told in confidence, Mrs. Davenport re-told it to her son, ending, "So now I understand why I have always sensed that she disliked you!"

"My dear mother!" he protested. "Surely it's a bit far-fetched to say that she dislikes *me* because some other fellow treated her badly!"

"Oh, not only you! When a woman has been badly hurt by one man, her reaction nine times out of ten is to distrust and fear all men for some considerable time. With Verity it has gone very deep indeed, poor child. So deep that I'm afraid it will be many a long day before her attitude to men and love and marriage is restored to normal."

Could she have foreseen the far-reaching effect her last words were to have on two lives, they would never have been spoken. Unguessing at the part they were to play in shaping destiny, she changed the subject. "Now tell me about yourself! Have you had an interesting day?"

A letter from Rhodesia brought more details of the Staverley's return to England. They would be arriving a few days before Christmas—news that set Mrs. Bream demanding vast amounts of dried fruits, so that she might make an outsize Christmas cake, double the usual quantity of mincemeat, and a giant pudding twice the size of those already in her cupboard. Verity spent hours helping her to stone raisins and chop candied peel—"Nane o' thon naisty packaged peel gets into *my* kitchen, or ma name's no' Williamina Isabella Bream!"

The time flew by in happy preparations. Verity took Mrs. Davenport on several shopping expeditions before the shops were overcrowded; Barclay let them have his car and chauffeur, going himself by taxi on his own affairs. Soon the spare bedroom overflowed with crackers, boxes of glacé fruits, long tinsel streamers and glass baubles for the tree, mysterious packages and parcels, scarlet wrapping paper gaily patterned, silver cord to tie it with.

For Jill, her mother bought a guilted dressing gown, nylons and filmy underwear, a cashmere twin set, soft and warm as thistledown. For John, a chunky pullover, sheepskin gloves, a giant box of marrons glacés, cigarettes. For Julia, a doll whose trousseau might have been the envy of any little girl—pleated skirt and twin set, meant for morning wear, blue woollen frock for afternoons, a party frock of primrose organdie, two coats, nightdress and dressing gown and bedroom slippers, three pairs of shoes, even a tiny pair of gumboots. A complete set of the Beatrix Potter books. A copy of *The Wind in the Willows*. And all manner of charming trifles the adoring grandmother had been unable to resist—a miniature hot water bottle, a doll's telephone no bigger than a thimble, a brush and comb of palest pink enamel, a washing machine barely a foot in height, that really worked.

Christmas cards were there in piles, waiting to be addressed, and presents to be parcelled up for friends outside the household. Mrs. Davenport wanted all the preparations finished before the travellers arrived, so that when she had them with her no time need be spent on anything that might be done in advance. So every evening after dinner she and Verity would set to work, addressing envelopes, writing labels, wrapping and addressing parcels. It was the happiest time of Christmas preparations Verity had known since the arrival of Nurse Kilsallow at Bleydon.

Late one afternoon Dr. Gairloch dropped in towards six o'clock. Ostensibly she came to have a chat with Mrs. Davenport, but Verity suspected that she knew this was the time when Barclay joined his mother for an hour or so. As Verity was gathering up her sewing, preparatory to quietly withdrawing, Barclay Davenport himself appeared. He murmured as he passed her on his way to greet the visitor, "Don't go. Stay and have a glass of sherry with us."

Verity would have preferred to leave them, but the words came as a command, rather than a invitation, and in a way he was her employer. Reluctantly she put her sewing on a chair and joined him by the table where the sherry waited. Silently he filled the glasses. Taking one, she carried it to Dr. Gairloch, put a small table by her side, then, as she was smoking, brought an ashtray—services that received no more thanks than a slight inclination of the sleek, greenish gold head, and an appraising glance of pale eyes.

Janice Gairloch wore a soft muted shade of green that emphasized her own strange greenish coloring. Silvery green eye shadow, cunningly applied, deepened and enlarged pale eyes. A faint exotic scent hung round her in a haunting aura. Verity was struck afresh by her distinction, her poised elegance, infinitely more enviable than mere prettiness.

Since her immediate future was assured, she had felt justified in doing a little shopping on her own account. The older woman's glance of critical appraisal made her glad that she was wearing for the first time one of her purchases, a plainly tailored frock of fine tweed in deep, glowing sapphire. The color deepened a hint of blue in her grey eyes, and was becoming to her light brown hair and fair skin; the knowledge that she looked her best gave her a confidence she badly needed.

Dr. Gairloch had taken a chair by Mrs. Davenport. Beside her was a vacant space, and beyond that a third chair by the fire. Barclay motioned Verity to the empty chair, handed her a glass of sherry, and drew up a fourth chair for himself into the vacant place.

Four is normally a pleasant number for a chat beside the fire upon a winter's afternoon. But in next to no time Janice Gairloch had skillfully transformed that number to a trio, so manoeuvring the conversation as to make a closed triangle between Barclay and his mother and herself, talking entertainingly of matters in which she must have known it was impossible for the younger girl to join, enveloping the three of them in a calculating intimacy from which she deliberately excluded Verity, ignoring her as though she were not there.

Silently she drank her sherry. Though she had no wish to be excluded in the talk, none the less the situation was embarrassing, making her feel gauche, although her exclusion was no fault of hers. Barclay reached out a shapely hand to flick away his cigarette ash. It caught her eyes and held them. Always she was fascinated by those hands of his, broad and muscular of palm, with long, strong fingers, hard as steel, yet sensitive as any woman's. She tried to picture them at work. But they would be concealed by rubber gloves, of course, and he would wear an overall and mask. Yet even among half a dozen others in the same anonymous attire, that assured carriage would surely make him easy to identify . . .

Rising, he refilled the glasses, then deliberately turned to Verity, leaving his mother and the visitor to a tête-à-tête. Anger glinted in his eyes; she knew it was on her account. Arrogant and domineering he may be, she thought, but he does at least consider other people's feelings! Suddenly he ceased to be a stranger. They were linked together by an odd, indefinable bond of understanding.

He said in a low voice, deliberately inaudible to the others, "I wonder if you have any ideas for something I can give Mrs. Bream and Ellen? I would prefer to give them something one had taken the trouble to buy, rather than money."

Verity could sense that Dr. Gairloch was straining her ears to hear what passed between them. To heighten the impression that they were discussing something confidential, she answered in the same low voice, "I know Mrs. Bream wants a new cardigan. A blue one. And Ellen is pining for a pair of sheepskin boots. I could find out the sizes, if you like?"

"H'm . . . I don't know that I can picture myself choosing cardigans and sheepskin boots! And then there's Mary Pridham, and my secretary. . . . D'you think you could find time to do a bit of shopping for me?"

"Of course! One afternoon, when Mrs. Davenport is resting. That is, if you don't mind who 'takes the trouble' to buy their presents?"

"Touché!" he said, and they both burst out laughing.

Dr. Gairloch rose, and the others followed suit. "I must go. Barclay, will you dine with me one night next week? I want to ask a very interesting couple I met in New York to meet you."

The temporary bond was broken. Once again they had become strangers, poles apart, as though the moment of intimacy linking them had never been.

Barclay said, " Thanks very much. It sounds delightful." He seemed to mean it. Perhaps he liked his elegant colleague. They must have a great deal in common. His annoyance over her bad manners had perhaps been only momentary.

They fixed an evening for the dinner. Dr. Gairloch bade Mrs. Davenport a cordial good night, then turned to Verity. "Good night, Miss—er——"

In her pale eyes Verity saw naked hatred blazing for a brief illuminating moment. Hatred she would turn on any woman who might come between herself and Barclay Davenport, whom she wanted for her own; hatred enhanced by the failure of her first attempt to oust the girl whose presence she resented here, and aggravated further by the moments Barclay had spent with her in low-toned talk. Hatred that knew no scruples and would stop at nothing to attain its ends.

Reason told Verity that the older woman had no power to harm her. She had nothing to fear. And yet—and yet——!

"My dear, you're shivering!" said Mrs. Davenport, concerned.

"Somebody walked over my grave, that's all!" said Verity.

At last the waiting time was over. This very evening, the Staverleys were due at London Airport. Barclay was going to meet them. He would bring them here for dinner before driving them to the service flat he had engaged for them within a few minutes of Harley Street.

Shortly before he had to leave, he joined his mother and Verity. Mrs. Davenport was putting final touches to the bag for Jill, and Verity was wrapping up a pair of gloves she had knitted for Mrs. Bream.

Barclay was carrying a cardboard box. Opening it, he took out something dark and softly opulent, and held it up for their inspection. "I've been doing a spot of Christmas shopping for Jill. D'you think she will approve of this?"

"This" was a baum marten stole of three superb skins, dark and full and lustrous, perfect for wearing with a tailor-made. They exclaimed in admiration, and his mother cried, "She'll be enchanted with it. What woman wouldn't?"

"Good!—I must be off."

"So soon? Is there a fog?"

"Nohting to speak of. I wish you didn't look so tired, Mamma!"

"Not really tired. Only excited."

"Same thing, in your case!" He touched her shoulder in a light caress, and went, leaving the marten stole forgotten on a chair.

Mrs. Davenport took it up, and laid her cheek against its soft warmth. "Jill will be thrilled with this! Barry is so good to us.—Our story is a sort of variation on the Cinderella theme, you know, with Barry in the role of fairy godfather! I was left a widow with very little money indeed, when he was twelve and Jill was only seven. Life became one long unending struggle to bring them up and make ends meet. For years I worked as a receptionist in a hotel to keep our home together, as well as running it without help."

Verity waited, hoping Mrs. Davenport would tell her more. She did.

"Then Barry qualified, first of his year—went on to qualify in surgery—did brilliantly—became house surgeon at Darlingford Hospital—performed an emergency operation on a business tycoon who was staying in the town, a patient of Sir Lucas Danvers. Something very touch-and-go. Sir Lucas was impressed, and took him up; said he would send him patients if he came to London. So we took a chance, sold out our last remaining scrap of capital—

and now, seven years later, he has made his name, and Cabinet Ministers and film stars and nawabs come queuing to have him take out their appendixes and what-not!"

"Rather a dramatic story!" Verity murmured.

"Yes. . . . For Barry, half the satisfaction of success is that it gives him the ability to do such lovely things for Jill and me, giving us luxurious presents—" she touched the furs. "Making up to me in every way that money can, for the lean years behind us. Yet for himself he's not ambitious in a wordly sense. Achievement is what matters to him, not recognition.— Will you hide the furs away? He won't want Jill to see them till the proper day! Then we might listen to that broadcast from the Festival Hall."

Some time had passed when they were startled by the shrill intrusion of the telephone upon the brilliant delicacy of a Chopin sonata. Verity went to answer it; it stood on a small table in a corner of the room.

Barclay's voice said "Verity?"

"Yes!" The thought flashed through her mind that he had telephoned to tell them that the plane had been delayed through fog, or even diverted to another airport.

"Turn off the wireless. Say you can't hear properly— make some excuse." He sounded odd, abrupt and strained. A sick sense of foreboding took possession of her as, murmuring an apology to Mrs. Davenport, she did as he had told her. Her hand shook as she took up the receiver.

'I suppose my mother is within hearing? . . . Now listen.
This is vitally important. *You must be careful how you answer me!* Don't give the slightest sign that anything is wrong. Got that?"

"Yes." She braced herself, hand on the table, waiting for catastrophe to break.

He said, "There's been a ghastly accident. A crash landing. Ten dead."

She caught her breath, managed to turn the sound into a slight cough. Sharply he said, "For God's sake keep a grip on yourself!"

She made herself repeat "Yes!" as calmly as though he had been telling her to keep the fire up, or that the fog was clearing.

"The child has only a slight injury. I'll bring her back with me. But the others——" He broke off, then said with evident difficulty, "Both dead. My mother mustn't know of it till I get back to her. Tell her I rang up to say the plane has been delayed, and we shall be so much later than I thought that she had better go to bed instead of waiting up. As soon as she's in bed, ring Dr. Anderson, tell him what has happened, and get him to come round —he'd better by handy when I tell her. All clear?"

"Perfectly."

"Don't have the wireless on. Better do something to put her portable out of action. Warn Mrs. Bream, as well. It's certain to be on the news—that's chiefly why I telephoned. I hate to land all this on you. . . . I shall be back as soon as I can get to you. Under an hour, with any luck."

He had rung off. Replacing the receiver, Verity took a deep breath and prepared to face the nightmare hours ahead.

CHAPTER FOUR

LATER, LOOKING back on the next hour, Verity saw it as a series of disconnected scenes.

Her own hands, wrenching at a connection in the portable wireless, heedless that they might be wrecking it for ever in her haste to put it out of action.

Mrs. Bream's red face, convulsed by weeping as they made the beds in the spare room, one for small Julia, the other for Verity herself so that the child would not be alone.

Herself, hiding away in drawers and cupboards the heartless mockery of the Christmas glitter so that Barclay should not see it on returning: sparkling baubles for the tree that now would not be decked, parcels wrapped with loving care in gaily patterned paper, and labelled "Jill, with love from Mother," "John, with every good wish for the happiest of Christmases!"

Dr. Anderson, the heart specialist, arriving quietly, concerned and kind and grave.

Herself again, so numbed by shock as to feel strangely calm, repeating what she had already told him on the telephone, and adding that Mrs. Davenport, suspecting nothing more serious amiss than the delaying of the long awaited family reunion, had gone protestingly to bed, declaring that she would get up and put on her housecoat when the travellers at last arrived, "no matter what Barry may have to say about it!" — Telling him, "But she doesn't feel as well as she pretends. I saw her in the mirror, taking one of her special pills. Soon after that, as she seemed drowsy, I left her resting quietly. She often dozes for a little while after she's had one."

Afterwards she wondered whether Dr. Anderson had thought it odd that Mrs. Davenport should feel like dozing at a time of such exciting anticipation; she would have thought it strange herself if her reactions had not been numbed by shock.

Then came the sound that should have heralded such joy, the muted rumble of the lift . . . All her life long Verity would remember Barclay Davenport, standing in the doorway with a face of stone, holding in his arms a child wrapped in a rug. Her dark head lay against his shoulder. Silky fronds of hair partly concealed a dressing on her temple. Her eyes were closed, her lashes making silken fans upon the pale triangle of her face. Was she unconscious or asleep?

Barclay said, "My mother——?"

Quickly she told him, "She has no idea there's anything amiss beyond a slight delay."

"I'll go to her at once.—Good of you to come, Anderson."

"I am so terribly sorry for the reason that you want me."

Verity said, "Shall I put Julia to bed? Everything is arranged for me to sleep with her in the spare bedroom."

"Would you? I'll take her there. There's nothing much wrong with her. Only a nasty graze under the dressing, and she may be a bit shocked. They'd given her a sedative by the time I got to her."

Going ahead of Verity, he laid his burden carefully on one of the beds. The silken lashes fluttered. Dark eyes opened, blinking, and a small voice murmured, "Mummy?" Before either of them could reply, the eyes had closed again. Their owner drifted back to sleep.

"Shall I give her something if she wakes? Hot milk?"

"She won't wake properly. She'll sleep right through till morning. All she needs is warmth and quiet."

"There are two hot bottles in her bed. And I sleep very lightly. If she stirs I'll be awake at once."

"Bless you! You've managed splendidly. It's been the greatest help to know that you were with my mother."

The numbness was beginning to wear off. Tears pressed heavily behind her eyes as Verity said huskily, "I'm so— *sorry . . .*"

He was silent for a moment, as though he too found speech difficult. Then, saying, "I must go to my mother," he left her.

Carefully Verity began to undress the sleeping child. Blood was streaked across her cheek, and there was more blood on her grubby little hands. Verity had sponged her gently, and was putting her into a silk blouse of her own by way of nightdress, when Barclay's voice rang through the flat, loud even through the closed door.

"Anderson——!"

Shuddering, chilled to the bone although the room was warm, she knew intuitively, as certainly as though he had come to tell her in so many words, that Mrs. Davenport was dead.

Verity felt as though she had slept no more than a few minutes when she heard a small voice saying questioningly "Mummy?" and she woke to face the sorrow and the problems of another day.

Memories of last night crowded in upon her agonizingly. Leaving Julia asleep, she had gone to the kitchen to sponge and press the clothes the child had worn when she arrived so that they would be fit to wear till others had been bought. She had been thankful for the occupation. To do nothing while she waited would have been intolerable. There had followed comings and goings and the murmur of strange voices, muted in the passage, and at last silence.

Soup Mrs. Bream had made for the uneaten dinner was in a bowl in the refrigerator. While she had waited Verity had heated some, lacing it with sherry. She poured some in a warmed jug, put it on a tray she had in readiness with a cup and spoon, then went to look for Barclay. She had found him looking haggard and exhausted, scribbling something on a pad beside the telephone. For a moment he had stared at her blankly, as though he had forgotten her existence. At last he said, "Oh . . . it's you . . . Verity, my mother——"

"You needn't tell me. And it's no use my trying to tell you—how I feel. I've brought you some hot soup, and after that I'll make an omelet, if you like."

"I've had a drink, I don't want anything to eat."

Ignoring that, she had poured soup in the cup and put it in his hand, and he had taken it automatically, then held the cup for more. Now came the one alleviating memory among the tragic ones. He had said abruptly, "There's just one crumb of comfort in it all. My mother never knew — about the accident. She seemed to be asleep when I went in. As I went up to the bed her eyes opened, and she looked beyond me and said happily, 'Why, Jill! At last!' And then she—slept again."

As though to save her from the need for a rejoinder, he had gone on without a pause, "I shall have a good deal to attend to. Will you see that Julia's all right? And get her anything she needs? Clothes—toys—anything you feel she ought to have. I'll make out a cheque."

She had been incapable of answering. The stupefaction that had numbed her had worn off, and pain had gripped her with intolerable poignancy. Tears brimmed in her eyes, then began sliding down her face. Hastily she turned away and would have left him, but he had seen. He took her by the shoulders, turned her to face him, and took her in his arms.

So her last memory of the tragic hours of yesterday was of the man whom to begin with she had thought hard and grim and ruthless, comforting her as he would have comforted a grieving child, her face against his shoulder and his cheek against her hair.

The small voice was repeating "Mummy?"

"Mummy isn't here, darling. I'm going to look after you today." Verity got up, put on her dressing gown, and went over to the other bed. Dark grey eyes gravely regarded her from a small pale face.

"Are you Granny?"

"No. My name is Verity." What explanation could she make of the bewildering change in Julia's world? She said, "Granny and Mummy and Daddy have gone away together," adding, so that it might not sound too final, "for a holiday."

"Have they gone camping? Last time they went camping Daddy shot a lion. Has Unkoo Barry gone too?"

"No. He's here. You'll see him presently."

To her relief the child seemed to have no memory of the accident. Probably it had all happened so suddenly and swiftly that there had been no time for fear before the crash, to leave an aftermath of frightening memories. And the blow upon her temple must have stunned her into merciful unconsciousness until the rescuers administered the sedative. A small thin hand with baby dimples on the knuckles came from beneath the bedclothes and cautiously explored the dressing. "My head hurts when I touch it, like the time when I fell off the verandah 'n' Mummy wasn't there 'n' Daddy took the new dress she was sewing me to wipe away the blood 'n' Mummy said to him, 'You've rooned the dress what I were making Julia so now you'll have to make her one your own self!' But she were only joking. Daddy can't sew. And he can't cook neither, except only fudge 'n' eggs 'n' bacon!" She looked about her with a puzzled expression. "How did I get here?"

"Uncle Barry brought you, late last night, after you had gone to sleep."

The answer seemed to rouse no memories of what had happened. "I'll get up now," she said.

Verity had meant to keep her quietly in bed till her uncle had seen how she was. But Julia had already scrambled up, a comic little figure, lost in the blouse that had served as an emergency nightdress. "Goodness, this is a funny sort of nightie I've got on!"

A knock came on the door and Mrs. Bream appeared, red-eyed but otherwise her normal self. "So the wee girlie's wakened! Ellen thought she heard you speaking. Are you ready for your breakfast, dearie?"

"Yes, please, after I've got on my clothes."

Verity said they would be ready in about twenty minutes.

"I'll have it waiting on you then. Mr. Davenport's away. He bade me tell you he'll be busy the whole day, he has things to see to and appointments that he can't put off, but he'll be back at six and there's no need for you to touch the dressing"—looking at Julia she touched her own forehead—"it can wait for him to see to it himself. He's left a cheque for you to get what's needed for the girlie."

41

Soon after they had breakfast Verity put on her outdoor things, then got the little coat Julia had arrived in. In spite of all her careful sponging, a dark stain still marked the front and there were spots on one sleeve. Julia said reproachfully, "It's dirty! Mummy doesn't like me wearing dirty clothes!"

"Something must have got spilt on it in the plane. We're going out now to get a new one for you, and some other things too."

It was a lovely morning. They would walk the short way to the shops in Oxford Street. With a strange sense of unreality Verity set out, holding Julia's hand, the little girl pattering sedately at her side.

This time yesterday, she thought, Mrs. Davenport and I were discussing what to give them for their first meal in England. And now . . . It *can't* be true! It simply can't have happened! . . . But it had. This was a nightmare that would not end in wakening.

Never before had she gone shopping for a child, but she had some idea of what to buy from the small garments Julia was wearing, and the shop assistants helped her with suggestions and advice. As she made her choices, Verity was thinking all the while of Mrs. Davenport, and what she would have chosen for her grandchild.

"I don't believe she'd like that color for a child. . . . She'd love this, I shall get it if they have it in the right size. . . . I wonder if she would have chosen the blue dressing gown or the pink one?"

Finally she bought a coat of fawn tweed in a bird's eye pattern with a neat velvet collar and a matching velvet cap, a little pleated skirt of the same tweed, a cosy twin set, shoes, nightdresses, everything a little girl could need for the next few days. They left the stained coat to be cleaned, and Julia, very pleased with herself, left the shop wearing the new one. All the other things would be delivered by this evening.

Last of all they visited a toyshop, where Julia, after long consideration, chose a baby doll two inches long, complete with bath and tiny sponge.

"This afternoon we'll make a bed for him out of a little box I've got," Verity told Julia.

"It isn't a him. It's a her and its name's Rosie. It'll need some clothes too, pore lickle thing!"

"I'll make some," Verity promised her, "and sheets too. I'll cut up a handkerchief. And a tiny pillow, stuffed with cottonwool."

The rapture on the small face beside her comforted her, as she thought how wonderful it was to give such pleasure with so little trouble.

In the first days following the tragedy, grief dulled Verity's ability to think clearly. Several days went by before she began to wonder about Julia's future.

Until now, she had had very little to do with children, and to begin with she had loved the child not for herself, but as the cherished grandchild of the woman who had been her friend, mingled with compassion for the tragic loss of which as yet she was serenely unaware.

But Julia's endearing little ways were irresistible. Verity's feelings swiftly deepened from kindliness and pity to a passion of protective tenderness, until she couldn't bear the thought of parting from her, of never seeing any more the flashing smile that lit her small grave face when something pleased her, nor her little hands, carefully tucking "Rosie" in her cardboard bed. And most unbearable of all was the thought of handing over Julia to some unloving stranger. Of her own uncertain future she would not think till Julia's was decided.

She found herself wondering and worrying continually as to what plans Barclay Davenport might be making for his small niece. When the funeral was over, she hoped that he might find the time to talk it over with her, but they met only for brief occasional glimpses. This was chiefly her own fault. She took her dinner on a tray to the room that had been hers before she moved into the spare room so as to be with Julia, and when he appeared shortly before Julia's bedtime, she left the two of them alone together. Once or twice Dr. Gairloch joined them, and Verity wondered whether he had asked her help in making plans for Julia. Anxiously she hoped not. She was convinced that Dr. Gairloch would not see Julia as a vulnerable little girl, but as a Case, with a capital C.

Two days before Christmas, going to fetch Julia to bed, she found her and her uncle sitting on the floor, "Building a house for Rosie out of books!" Julia explained.

Verity asked Barclay whether he could spare her a few minutes after Julia had gone to bed.

"Of course. You had better abandon your unsociable habits and have dinner with me."

"Oh, there's no need for that! All I have to say won't take five minutes."

"I want to discuss something that will take considerably longer. Will you tell Ellen we will dine together, or shall I?"

After that it would have been ungracious to persist in her refusal, so she said that she would tell the housemaid when she brought Julia's milk and biscuit. Was he going, she wondered, to tell her what he had decided about Julia's future?

She did not join him by the fire when Julia was in bed, but waited until Ellen came to tell her dinner was ready. She found Barclay waiting for her in the dining-room.

This was the first time she had been alone with him since she had broken down and wept against his shoulder. The memory embarrassed her; she hoped he had forgotten it. His manner was pleasantly impersonal, but none the less shyness made her hesitant as she said, "Tomorrow is Christmas Eve. I wonder—would you simply hate it if Julia and I put up some decorations? One can't feel festive. But I thought perhaps you wouldn't mind, for Julia's sake. Christmas does matter so much to a child. . . ."

"Good heavens! Of course I don't mind. I should have suggested it myself. Poor scrap, of course she's got to have a proper Christmas. What about presents, and a turkey, and crackers, and so on?"

"Her presents have been all wrapped up and ready for the last three weeks. And all the rest is laid on, too."

"We must have midday dinner, obviously, because of Julia."

'We . . ." So he meant to have it with them?

"Do you mind? Will it be inconvenient?"

"Not at all. Only I have a date to carve the turkey in the women's surgical ward at St. Michael's, complete with

44

chef's hat, and merry quips, and mistletoe in every doorway, so I can't be with you much before two. D'you think you and Julia can endure the pangs of hunger all that time?"

"She can have elevenses. Or perhaps twelvses would divide the morning better!"

"Does she often ask about her parents?"

"She often speaks of them. 'Mummy says this' or 'Daddy does that' and tells me things that happened. But she doesn't seem to worry about when they're coming back. From what she says, I gather she was used to being left with friends from time to time while they were away from home."

"They used to go off on safari when John had short leave, filming wild animals, so providentially she's used to being without them now and then. Otherwise she would have fretted for them, poor baby! . . . I must decide on some plan for her upbringing, at any rate for the next year or two. I want to talk it over with you, when we've settled down to have our coffee." He changed the subject, but returned to it when they were sitting by the fire, the coffee on a tray between them.

"About Julia. Have you any suggestions? Any ideas for possible arrangements I might make for her?"

Verity said slowly, "Nothing very definite. I've no experience of children. But I do feel very strongly that above all you should aim at giving her a feeling of security, and of being loved. Of—of *mattering*. . . ."

"Love and a sense of security are the two first essentials every child needs," said Barclay drily. Verity felt that she had stated something obvious as though it were original, but felt better as he went on, "Unfortunately, far too many people fail to realize it. Instincts become atrophied through lack of use, and no amount of intellect can take their place.—As I see it, there are two alternatives for Julia. One would be to send her to a small nursery school where she would be with children of her own age. The other, to keep her here, in charge of someone who would love her for her own sake—not just care for her conscientiously, as a job to be punctiliously carried out. What d'you think about it?"

She cried, "Oh, *please* do keep her here! In even the very best of nursery schools she couldn't be an individual in the same way as if she stays with you. Here she'll take root—she'll grow up feeling she belongs—that this is home."

Barclay was silent, gazing thoughtfully at the cigarette he held between two long fingers. Verity went on, "I'm sorry if I sound rather emotional about it! But Julia is so responsive and affectionate and—and sensitive, that I've been worrying about her rather badly. Somehow she seems particularly vulnerable."

Barclay said quietly, "I don't think you sound at all 'emotional.' I had already reached the same conclusion as yourself, and asked for your opinion, wondering whether your reactions were the same as mine. Now for the next step. If I keep Julia here, will you take charge of her?"

"*I*——?"

"You sound surprised."

"I am!" Longing to accept this solution, not only of Julia's future but of her own as well, she hesitated before accepting it. "I've already told you I have no experience of children. Do you really mean it? Do you think I should be suitable?"

"If I hadn't thought so, I should scarcely have suggested it," he pointed out. "You have common sense. Your instincts seem to be in first-class working order. Admirable guides! And you yourself said that above all Julia needs a feeling of security, and of being loved. Already you have given her both these things. Their continuity would be invaluable. Take your time to think it over. Let me know what you've decided in a week or so."

Verity was considering the problems that might be involved. For one thing, it was obvious that Barclay Davenport would not want to have his life entangled with a nursery régime, although he might not care to say so, in so many words. She must take care to make it plain from the beginning that her own wish, as well as his, was for a completely separate existence.

"If I stay," she said, "some reorganizing will be necessary, won't it?"

"Such as——?"

"Might I turn the room I used to have into a nursery? Julia will need a playroom. And we could have meals there. And I could sit there, in the evenings."

"As you please. We should have to arrange for you to have some free time regularly. Ellen, or perhaps Mary Pridham, might take charge of Julia."

"Thank you! It might be a good thing if something of the sort can be arranged occasionally. But I shan't want free time regularly, I haven't any friends in London."

"It sounds to me as though you don't want any time to think it over, after all!"

As their eyes met, she knew whence Julia had got the smile that suddenly would light her small grave face when something pleased her. Flushing a little, she smiled back at him. "I think I knew I'd stay as soon as you suggested it. I had been simply dreading leaving Julia!" she confessed.

For Julia, Christmas was complete and utter bliss. On Christmas Eve her excitement and delight made well worth while the decorating of the rooms with holly and pretty glittering baubles that to her uncle and Verity seemed mockery of what might have been. Long before daylight, Verity was awakened by a small voice that implored her, "Can we have the light on, so's I can unpack my stocking?"

The opening of the larger presents was postponed till after breakfast, by the fireplace where she found them stacked. "Pore Father Christmas! I expected he were too tired to bring them any farther, with all the work he had to do last night!" said Julia sympathetically. Verity had re-labelled some of the presents bought for her by Mrs. Davenport so as to make it seem they were her parents' gifts: discussing it with Barclay, they had agreed it would be time enough when she had grown accustomed to their absence, to explain that they would not be returning.

Verity sat by Julia on the floor, helping to undo difficult knots, and tidying the accumulating litter into the waste paper basket as one treasure after another was revealed, while Barclay sat astride a chair, arms folded on the back of it, silently looking on. When everything had been unwrapped and Julia was blissfully making imaginary tea for Rosie in her tiny teaset, he took a box that lay beside him on the floor, and handed it to Verity.

Opening the lid, she saw furs lying amid layers of tissue paper. "Take it out and have a look," he told her.

Verity took up an exquisite cape stole of sables, luxury incarnate. She turned it this way and that, smiling and sighing at its rich soft loveliness. "It's simply beautiful! How very kind of you to think of giving it to me! But I can't possibly accept it."

"What am I to do with it, if you don't?"

"Surely there must be someone else—someone more suitable—you'd like to have it."

"No one, I assure you. Put it on."

She did as she was told. The furs caressed her, flattering her, cherishing her, soft and light and warm. She sighed again, and shook her head. "I can't take this, honestly. Besides, I'd never have an opportunity of wearing it."

" 'Never is a long word,' they say. One never knows what may be waiting round tomorrow's corner! Take it. You can't refuse it, if you look upon it as a legacy from my mother."

So she hung the furs upon a padded hanger in her wardrobe, promising herself that she would never use them. One day they should be Julia's. Meanwhile from time to time she put them on, luxuriating in their cherishing caress, gazing wistfully at her glamorous reflection, knowing she would never in her life own anything that suited her so well. Often she wondered why it was that Barclay Davenport had given her the stole. Surely there must be some woman, or even women, in his life who would have been enchanted by such a gift?

Christmas over, life soon settled into its new pattern. After breakfast Julia would play contentedly while Verity did the housekeeping. After that, if it were reasonably fine they would go out, sometimes to see the Changing of the Guard, sometimes to feed the ducks in one or other of the parks. After lunch in the new playroom Julia would rest while Verity sewed, or did the ironing, or any other necessary chores. There would follow another short walk, then tea, then Verity would read aloud of Toad and Rat and Mole, till at the sound of footsteps heavier than Mrs. Bream's or Ellen's, Julia would rush joyfully to welcome back her uncle, who unfailingly returned to spend an hour with her before she went to bed. Verity saw very little of him nowadays. They met briefly when she went to fetch Julia to bed, and once a week at lunch on Sunday, which Barclay had decreed that they should all three have together in the dining-room. To his small niece he was charming, talking to her gravely as one adult to another. To Verity his manner, always pleasant, was impersonal and detached.

January was half gone when one day after lunch, as Verity was ironing while Julia rested on her bed, Mrs. Bream appeared.

"You're wanted on the telephone."

"*I* am?" Verity stared at her in astonishment. "But I don't know a single soul in London. Who can it be?"

Mrs. Bream sniffed. "Her on the first floor. I kent her voice although she didna give her name."

Dr. Gairloch! Verity's feeling of foreboding in connection with the psychiatrist had gradually died away. Now it returned in full force, filling her with apprehension, as going to the telephone she said, "Verity Cator speaking."

A cold clear voice said in her ear, "This is Dr. Gairloch. There is something I must discuss with you, Miss Cator. How soon can you make it convenient to spare me a quarter of an hour?"

Verity did some rapid thinking. She would be free while Julia was with her uncle before she went to bed. If by some chance he was delayed, Ellen or Mrs. Bream would gladly keep an eye on the little girl.

"I can be free at six o'clock, if that will suit you?"

"I will make it suit me. I shall expect you here at six. Good-bye!"

Slowly Verity replaced the receiver. What did that cold, incalculable woman on the first floor want of her? Impossible to guess. Yet every instinct warned her that the interview would be unpleasant. Apprehension grew, as she went back to finish ironing Julia's nightdress.

CHAPTER FIVE

A SALLOW black-haired woman, wearing a white overall, opened the door when Verity arrived punctually at six o'clock at the flat on the first floor. Saying unsmilingly, "Miss Cator? The doctor is expecting you, but a patient has delayed her. She will be with you soon," she showed the visitor into a large empty room and left her to her own devices.

Dr. Gairloch's drawing-room was comfortably warm, yet as she looked about her Verity felt chilled. Two standard lamps had parchment shades whose white was faintly tinged with green, so that their light had a peculiarly under-water effect. No book left lying open, no needlework or knitting nor half-folded daily paper gave the room an air of human occupation. All was impersonal perfection. The décor might have been completed yesterday by some professional hand. Dead white walls and woodwork were immaculate. Curtains of celadon green hung in shimmering sculptured folds. The lilac damask covers of the chairs, the matching velvet of the Knole settee, looked as unused as new stock in the showroom of an expensive store. Over the chimneypiece hung an ultra-modern painting framed in glistening white, depicting, on a background of mauve and purple cubes and triangles broken by one or two black zigzag lines, a pale green predatory hand reaching downward from the top left hand corner towards a disembodied mouth that pouted up at it some two-thirds down the curious composition. As Verity was staring at it with a puzzled frown, wondering what, if anything, it was supposed to represent, she heard the door behind her opening, and turned to find herself face to face with Dr. Gairloch.

Today Janice Gairloch wore black. Verity realized that probably she wore it as a kind of working uniform, as a man doctor wears a dark suit, but there was something workaday in the sheath of soft soot-black material that clung to breast and thigh and slender waist. There were jade ear-rings in her small flat ears, and a jade ring on one long white hand. Her sleek hair moulded her head like a close-fitting cap of green-gold satin. Verity marvelled that her narrow face, pale as a magnolia, showed no trace of weariness after a day spent in delving into other people's sick and suffering minds, which surely must be an exhausting business . . . unless, of course, one could remain detached, one's mind involved, but not one's sympathies?

Janice Gairloch's eyes, shallow and cold as glass, flickered over Verity, met her eyes briefly, finally rested on her mouth. She did not ask her to sit down, although she offered her a slender black-enamelled cigarette case. "No?" Taking one herself, she fitted it in a long jade holder, and lit it, all the while gazing at her visitor. ("As if I were a rabbit and she was a weasel, trying to hypnotize me!" Verity reflected later.)

She said, "I don't wish to detain you, so I will come straight to the reason why I asked you here. Tell me: is your flouting of the canons of society done in deliberate defiance of convention?"

Verity stared at her inquisitor in dumbfounded silence. "Flouting the canons of society"—"Defiance of convention." What *could* she be driving at?

The metallic voice went on, "Or is it possible that you are so completely lacking in sophistication that you fail to realize that your behaviour must give rise before long to highly undesirable gossip—if it has not already done so?"

It dawned at last on Verity that she was referring to the situation between Verity herself and Barclay Davenport. Feeling her face grow hot with anger, she could only hope that Dr. Gairloch would not conclude that she had blushed because she was ashamed.

"I am unaware," she said, "of anything unsuitable in my behaviour. Do you mean that busybodies might gossip because I live unchaperoned under the same roof as Mr. Davenport?"

"What else? I should have thought it obvious."

"Obvious? I'm afraid I don't agree. It's utterly preposterous! Good gracious—I'm no more to him than Mrs. Bream or Ellen!"

The thin lips twisted spitefully. "My dear girl—I know him well enough to realize that without your telling me! You are of course, the very last type to appeal to him. To anyone who understands him, it's obvious that he asked you to take charge of Julia simply because it happened to be convenient, and because to him you are so lacking in attraction that the possibility of scandal never entered his head."

"Nor anybody else's head, I should have thought unless it's occupied by a particularly nasty mind!" retorted Verity with spirit. "I spend my time in looking after Julia and running the flat. If I exchange more than half a dozen words with Mr. Davenport in the course of a day, which isn't often, they concern either the housekeeping or Julia's welfare. The most malicious gossip can't find anything amiss with that. Besides, surely my reputation is my own affair!"

"*Yours,* yes." Her tone implied that Verity was such a nonentity as to be of not the slightest interest to anyone. "But Mr. Davenport's is quite another matter. He is at the top of his profession. In his position, the slightest hint of scandal in his private life would be disastrous."

"Surely his reputation as a surgeon is what affects his patients—not his private life!"

"Few men would trust their womenfolk to a man of doubtful moral character. . . . I consider it my duty, as an old friend of Mr. Davenport, to point out to you that you are doing him a grave disservice in allowing the present situation to continue."

"I should have thought that Mr. Davenport was entirely capable of looking after his own interests."

" 'Men are unwise, and curiosly planned!' Few men care to admit that they have been mistaken in some course of action, when eventually they come to realize it. If his mistake in this particular instance were to be pointed out to him I have no doubt whatever that he would deny it. To retrieve the situation must be your own responsibility."

"You mean I ought to leave?"

"Can you consider staying, when you reflect on the effect your presence in such unconventional circumstances is bound to have on Mr. Davenport's reputation, and his future?"

I was right, thought Janice Gairloch, staring with narrowed eyes at Verity's expressive face. She is in love with him, although she may not know it yet. She would have stayed, regardless of her own reputation, but Barclay's is another matter to her.

"But Julia——" said Verity slowly.

"Julia will be just as happy in the care of someone else, or in some small school where she would be with other children." She's weakening! thought Dr. Gairloch. She's wavering. At first I thought that she was going to be difficult. But she's going to give in, after all. Ash fell unheeded from her cigarette on to the smooth perfection of the carpet as she said, "When you tell Mr. Davenport that you are leaving, you will of course prevaricate as to the reason."

"Why should I? Why not tell the truth?"

"You must remember that it is my business to know human nature inside out. Pride is one of Barclay Davenport's most outstanding characteristics. He would so resent the implication that unpleasant gossip could affect him, that I have no doubt he would pooh-pooh the whole idea and talk you into staying — even though subconsciously he would know that such a course must ultimately be disastrous."

She didn't get me here simply to tell me all this out of concern for Barclay, Verity reflected. This is simply another way of trying to get rid of me. And yet—and yet, what if there *should* be some truth in what she says?

"I must go," she said. "It's Julia's bedtime."

The older woman's cool poise as she said good night made her own abruptness appear crude and gauche by contrast.

When she had gone, Janice Gairloch went to a cocktail cabinet made out of an old lacquer chest, and poured herself a glass of Tio Pepe, the only sherry she enjoyed, since she disliked sweetness in a drink, as in all other things. For a few minutes she sat sipping it, and considering the scene just ended. She was almost sure that it would work out as she had planned. The girl was full of all the qualities that got one nowhere: unselfish, scrupulous, idealistic, suffering from an overdeveloped conscience. She knew the type.

Still, "almost" wasn't good enough. She must make sure. Perhaps a word with Barry . . . twisting the situation so that he would see it from another angle? What if each should find that she had spoken of it to the other— and what she had said? Still, that was most improbable. She would take the risk. "Nothing venture, nothing win."

Presently she went to her room and changed into a housecoat of jade green velvet. She touched up her lips, powdered her narrow face afresh, sprayed herself with the dry, exotic scent she favored. Then she went to the telephone and dialled the number of the flat above.

"Barry? I should be interested to hear your views on the judgment in that case of the house surgeon versus the hospital. Why not come down and have a cocktail with me, if you have half an hour to spare? . . . Yes, right away. Good!"

As she replaced the receiver Janice Gairloch's lips curved in a slow secretive smile, down-curving at the corners in a way that made her look as though she were sneering . . . which, in fact, she often was.

"God bless Mummy'n' Daddy'n' Verity'n' Unkoo Barry'n' Mrs. Bream'n' Ellen'n' help Mrs. Bream to find her spectacles 'n' make Ellen's corns better'n' make tomorrow a fine day so's me'n' Verity can go to the Zoo and help me to be a good girl for Jesus' sake Amen!" said Julia, and scrambled into bed.

Verity bent over her. A pair of skinny little arms came up and clasped her round the neck. She kissed a small face soft and sweet as petals, and was enveloped in the innocent odors of soap, and milk, and clean linen.

"Good night, darling!"

"G'night. See you in the morning!" said Julia sleepily, as she settled down to think about tomorrow's expedition to the Zoo.

Verity went quietly away and began tidying the bathroom. As she hung the bathmat and Julia's pink fleecy towel on the radiator, wiped the bath, and put a floating swan and a whole fleet of little ducks out of sight in a cupboard, for the first time she began trying to sort out all that Dr. Gairloch had said. To think coherently had been impossible while she was putting Julia to bed.

She didn't get me down there out of anxiety to be helpful! Verity decided. She did it in the hope of getting rid of me. She'd stick at nothing to get Barclay for herself, and sees me as an obstacle, although she said herself that I'm the last type to appeal to him—and goodness knows he's made that obvious! But probably she would be jealous of any woman he had anything to do with. And that time she came up for sherry, and her bad manners to me drove him into taking far more notice of me than he would otherwise have done, may have misled her into thinking that he likes me.

Is there any truth in what she said about my staying here, now Mrs. Davenport is dead, being a cause for gossip? How could anybody know about it unless he tells them—or Dr. Gairloch herself? And even if it does become known, no one who knows him would imagine there was anything—unconventional—about it! . . . But I suppose one must consider all the possible patients who don't know him personally, and might be misled by gossip. . . .

If only there were someone she could go to for advice, someone experienced in the ways of the world she could consult! But there was no one. She must make her mind up for herself. Torn this way and that, she left her dinner tray almost untouched, and had to put some of its contents in a little parcel she would burn, so that Mrs. Bream should not be affronted by the return of her unfinished helpings.

The thought of leaving Julia was unendurable. The little girl had wound herself about her heart as sweet pea tendrils cling to their supporting stake. Julia returned her love, trusted her, depended on her . . . Yet one must remember that no one was indispensable! She knew that if she were to leave, Julia would be bitterly distressed. . . Or would she accept Verity's departure in the same way that she had taken the absence of her parents, be content to think she would return before long, get what she needed of security and love from Verity's successor?

Was she really risking Barclay Davenport's reputation by remaining here? Or was it all a spiteful storm in a teacup? In any case, he was perfectly capable of taking good care of his own interests . . . unless through stubborn pride he should cut off his nose to spite his face. And she had loved his mother. . . .

Taking up the small blue cardigan she was knitting for Julia, Verity wished she knew what she should do. Things were so simple when one was in the nursery and schoolroom; conscience told one this was right and that was wrong and there were no two ways about it! What a pity that the grown-up world became so complicated and confusing.

Perhaps after I've slept on it, she thought, the tangle will have sorted itself out.

However, morning brought her no solution, and when Ellen gave her a message that Mr. Davenport would be obliged if she would have dinner with him this evening, her reaction was to think that he himself had realized belatedly the drawbacks to the present situation, and was going to break it to her that he must make other arrangements for Julia.

All day she felt on edge, tense and suspenseful. When Julia's bedtime came, and Verity went to fetch her from her usual playtime with her uncle, she shot a swift glance at Barclay, wondering instinctively, although absurdly, whether his face would give some clue to his thoughts. The eyes that met her own were as inscrutable as ever.

When Julia was tucked up in bed, Verity went to her own room to get ready for dinner. Convinced the moment was approaching when she would be tactfully, kindly, but firmly given notice, she realized afresh, with a sick heart, how much she dreaded leaving, how deeply she had grown to love not only Julia, but the house in Harley Street itself, how fond she had become of Mrs. Bream and Ellen, how much she felt herself part of the pattern of life here: so much so, that she would even regret saying good-bye to Barclay Davenport himself, aloof and baffling, hard to understand as he had proved.

Time enough to face the worst when it had happened. Meanwhile, she must concentrate on hiding how she felt. She wouldn't let him see how much she minded when the blow fell. She would go down with flying colors and her pride unscathed, no matter how her heart was suffering behind a brave façade of smiling acquiescence! To stiffen her morale she wore her prettiest frock, one that she had bought to wear on Christmas night . . . that tragic Christmas night when grief had taken the place of the anticipated gaiety. It was of leaf-green chiffon, soft and frail, with sleeves that at her elbows fell away into long floating wings. A bit too much, just for an ordinary everyday meal at home with one's employer! she decided, staring at her reflection. But I don't care. I'm going to need every scrap of help that I can get to keep my courage up, and this is quite the most becoming frock I've ever had . . . though I suppose after tonight I'll hate the sight of it. Oh, hurry hurry, Time, and get this over!

While she waited she began rehearsing little sentences. "Oh yes, indeed, of course I see your point of view. In any case, I always felt it was a purely temporary arrangement."

"From my own point of view, I'm glad you've come to that decision. After a more spacious existence in the country, I've been feeling life here very——" What was the word she wanted? Circumscribed? Constricted?

Ellen had come to tell her dinner was ready.

At first they talked of Julia. Presently Barclay began telling Verity of Jill and John, Jill's gaiety, John's steady kindliness, and of how happy they had been together. "One must try to keep their memories alive in Julia's mind," he said, "although as she's so young, poor scrap, it mayn't be easy."

"One"—not "we." Yes—there was no doubt, no doubt at all, that he was going to tell her she must go!

Last time they had drunk coffee together by the fire, Barclay had asked her whether she would stay on here and care for Julia. Handing him his coffee, Verity wondered whether he, too, remembered that; whether he was at all concerned as to what her feelings would be when he gave her notice, or her future, when she left.

He was behaving in a manner most unlike his usual calm self-possession. Silently he stirred his coffee, but did not drink it, poked the fire, which had no need of his attentions, took out his cigarette case, opened it, then shut it and returned it to his pocket.

Verity felt she couldn't bear this artificial situation any longer. Better far to clear the air between them. She would lay her cards upon the table, and be done with it! She said impulsively, "Look—I've got a pretty good idea of what you're trying to say! Dr. Gairloch rang up yesterday and said that she must see me about something urgent. So I went down and had a session with her while Julia was with you. She left me in no doubt at all of what she thinks about my living here—*and* of what everybody else will think and say about it! I imagine she's been saying the same sort of thing to you?"

"She has indeed!" He smiled at her—that sudden, charming smile he shared with Julia. His look of being ill at ease had gone, as he took out his abandoned cigarette and lit it. "I felt we'd better talk it over. I'd been wondering how on earth to put it to you. . . . I was summoned to a session on the subject last night, on another pretext while you were putting Julia to bed. Of course, it's pretty obvious that Janice's motives for her interference are far from being concern about your reputation, as she makes out. . . ."

"*My* reputation? It was *yours* that she went on about to me!"

Their laughter banished the last traces of the tension lingering between them. Barclay said thoughtfully, "All the same, it's no laughing matter! One must admit this is an unconventional set-up, though you and I know very well that the whole situation couldn't be more proper and correct if each of us were guarded day and night by a whole posse of Mrs. Grundys! I owe you an apology for asking you to put yourself in a position some people might consider compromising. In normal circumstances I might not have suggested it, but at the time that aspect of it didn't strike me. I was too distressed to think straight.

Julia was my one concern. Well, now—the thing is, what d'you want to do about it? How do you feel about the possibility of tittle-tattle?"

Verity said with spirit, "As far as I'm concerned, I couldn't care less! As I see it, it's all much ado about nothing. I don't know how you feel about it, though. Maybe from your point of view you want me to go?"

He shook his head. "The very last thing that I want."

"Then if that's how you feel, I'd like to stay. For Julia's sake. I feel that I can give her something. Something that she badly needs." She hesitated, then said, "For my own sake, too, I want to stay."

"Good! If that's the way you really feel about it, that's the way I want it, too. For all our sakes." He added, "We must bear in mind Janice Gairloch's attitude towards it all."

"But it's no concern of hers!" Verity protested.

Barclay's eyes, which had been frank and friendly, became enigmatic as he answered, "None whatever. But it is unwise to underestimate an adversary." Evidently unwilling to discuss Dr. Gairloch, he changed the subject. "I'm glad the day has ended up as well as it began. I had an anxious start, in more ways than one. This morning I did an operation I'd been dreading for some time. A Cæsarean for twins. The patient had a bad heart, too, and there were other complications. One way and another, it was obviously going to be touch and go."

"But it went off all right?"

"Yes. Very much all right. A boy and girl, and all three doing well. One of the better moments!" His smile was reminiscent; in his mind he saw again the father's face when he had heard that all was well, the mother on her pillows, in a drowsy seventh heaven of happiness, the crumpled crimson faces of the newborn.

"I suppose in time a doctor becomes impersonal and detached about his patients?"

"Some seem to. I often wish I could! To me, each of them remains a suffering human being—not just a piece of miraculous machinery. It can be painful, when one's emotions are involved . . . emotions one must never show. One learns to build up an impersonal manner, by way of a façade to screen them."

Verity began to understand the reason for his enigmatic manner, his aloof inscrutability that in the beginning had exasperated her. A shapely hand, its fingers sensitive yet strong as steel, reached out to flick his cigarette ash in the ashtray at his side. She watched it, fascinated, thinking of the miracles those hands of his had wrought, the tragedies they had averted, trying to picture that side of his existence that was hidden from her.

For a little time they talked. Presently, when silence fell, she rose to go. Barclay, his hand upon the handle of the door to open it paused. "There's one thing I should be very grateful if you'd do for me."

"Of course!" She waited, wondering why he seemed to find it difficult to say.

My mother's personal belongings, and those of Jill's that weren't destroyed. They must be gone through. I wonder if you would do it for me?"

She said again, "Of course I will! But you must tell me what you want done with them?"

"Jewellery—anything of that sort—can be kept for Julia. For the rest, you'll have to use your own discretion. Ellen might like any of mother's clothes that would be suitable—none of them would meet round Mrs. Bream!" He hesitated. "Your build is very much the same as Jill's. Will you take anything of hers that you could use? She used to have attractive things. I know she would be glad for you to have them."

Touched and embarrassed, she replied, "It's very kind indeed of you to think of it! But—you would hate to see me wearing anything of hers. . . ."

"I wouldn't even know it had been hers. You must remember that I haven't seen her for three years. Do what you think best with everything. I leave it all to you. No hurry—do it by degrees, when it's convenient."

She told him that she would, and said good night.

She found Julia fast asleep, her lashes making crescent shadows on her cheek. One small hand curled beneath her cheek, the other laid protectively on her favorite bedtime companion, a one-eyed teddy bear. Verity dropped on her knees beside her in a passion of relief and thankfulness that after all she need not leave her.

Later, lying wakeful, she re-lived the happenings of the evening, savouring again the ending of suspense on learning Barclay wanted her to stay, wondering why it was that in the passing of an hour or so her feelings towards him should have undergone such a drastic change, and going through the various phases of her attitude towards him since she came here.

In the beginning she had heartily disliked him. Gradually, as she came to know him better, dislike had merged into a reluctant respect. Later still, she had begun to like him, in a grudging sort of way. And now, tonight, suddenly she had been startled by her awareness of him as a man.

What was it that had brought about this last change in her attitude? Was it the sharing with him of a time of tragedy and crisis? Or his lowering of the façade of which he had spoken, the barrier deliberately raised to hide emotions he preferred to keep concealed? Or was it something else?

Again his deep voice echoed in her mind, telling her, "If that's the way you feel about it, that's the way I want it too. For all our sakes."

For all our sakes. . . . Not only so that she might stay with Julia, not only because it was her own wish to remain, but for his own sake as well.

"For all our sakes. . . ." Could there, in those four words, be some hint of his feelings for her? Had they altered, as her own for him had altered—so gradually that until now she had been unaware of it?

Impatiently she wrenched herself out of her dreaming and came down to earth. Don't be a sentimental goose! she told herself. He's bound to know a dozen girls far more attractive than you are! You don't mean any more to him than Mrs. Bream or Ellen. You're important to him for Julia's sake—no more than that.

Julia. . . . Darling, vulnerable little Julia. Oh, thank heaven that I haven't got to leave her, after all!

CHAPTER SIX

A FEW days after Verity and Barclay had agreed she should stay on in Harley Street, in spite of Dr. Gairloch's prophecies of gossip, Verity reluctantly began the task of going through Mrs. Davenport's belongings. She did it gradually, in the evenings, when Julia was in bed. Now and then she was obliged to consult Barclay over some decision, but as far as possible she avoided troubling him about it. He had suggested that the cousin who had lived with them before Verity came might like some personal momentoes, and to her she sent, with his approval, Mrs. Davenport's blue enamel toilet set, a pigskin bag and one of black suede, and several charming scarves. Otherwise there was no relative to be considered, so when Mrs. Bream and Ellen had been given everything that might be of use to them, she sent all that remained to the Vicar of a needy East End Parish.

When all had been disposed of and the drawers and cupboards were empty, Verity set to work to deal with Jill's belongings. That, too was painful, for though they had never met she had heard so much of her that she felt as though they had been friends. Fortunately very few of Jill's possessions had arrived here. She had brought little with her, meaning to buy new clothes when she got back to London, and of those that she had brought, much had been lost or spoilt in the plane crash. Verity's chief problem was what to do with the contents of several cardboard boxes that contained clothes she had never worn. Since Jill no longer had what she had worn last time she came home, nor any other garments suited to the London winter, these were presents from her mother, who had chosen them so that on arrival she would have an outfit ready to be worn at once. Verity, who had helped to choose them, knew exactly what was in the boxes, and without opening them she spoke of them to Barclay, going in search of him one evening after Julia was in bed.

She found him reading by the fire. She asked, "Can you spare five minutes to talk over something?"

Barclay rose. "Fifty, if you like! Have a glass of sherry with me?"

"Oh, no, thanks! I didn't mean to make a social occasion of it!" she protested, glancing down at the white overall she still wore after bathing Julia. Barclay paid no heed, but went to get the sherry.

When they were sitting, she in a chair beside the fire, he on a sofa facing it, Verity explained about the clothes. "Surely the shops your mother got them from would take them back, if I were to explain the circumstances?"

"Oh, Lord, no! One can't ask them to do that, particularly as my mother must have got them weeks ago. Can't you make use of them yourself? Your build is very much the same as Jill's."

Verity had felt it would be impossible for her to wear anything of Jill's, since Julia would recognize them. Already she had given some of her clothes to Mary Pridham, and the rest to Ellen for a niece. However, Julia would not associate these unworn garments with her mother. All the same . . . Still, better not prolong discussion of a painful subject by an argument!

"Well, yes, I could. But——"

"Then please do!" said Barclay, and brushed aside her embarrassed thanks by adding that there was no sense in letting the things get old-fashioned, or be eaten by the moths.

She hated saying what must follow, yet it must be done, although she knew it would remind him painfully of that happy evening when he had been about to start to meet the travellers from Rhodesia at London Airport, and looking in to tell his mother he was off, had shown her the baum marten stole that he had chosen for his sister's Christmas present— never dreaming it was the last time he would speak to her.

That stole you brought for Jill for Christmas—I'd forgotten it, until last night I found it in its box. Surely the furrier would take that back?"

"I wouldn't dream of asking him. You——"

Afraid he might be going to offer it to her, and anxious to prevent it, Verity said quickly, "In that case, shall I send it to your cousin?"

He shook his head emphatically. "She would have no use for it. She lives in tweeds. Hates what she calls 'bits and pieces'!"

Verity laughed at this description. "Honestly, one can't call that lovely stole either a 'bit' or a 'piece'!" she protested.

"That's as may be! Anyway, I do assure you Cousin Margaret would never wear the thing. So do please take it for yourself."

"But——" How was she to put it? "Don't you see, I *can't* accept such an expensive present from you! As it is, I feel uncomfortable about taking those lovely clothes of Jill's, all of them new."

"If you don't have them, what do you suggest that I should do with them? Send them to a jumble sale?" he asked impatiently. Obviously, and quite naturally, the subject was to him as painful as it was embarrassing to her. In the circumstances, one couldn't go on arguing about it. Willy-nilly, she must accept all that he wanted her to take, and talk of other topics. "If that's really how you feel about it, thank you very much indeed. I could never have afforded anything so lovely for myself! And now there's something else that has been bothering me. Wouldn't it be a good thing for Julia to have an opportunity of meeting other children?"

"Odd that you should mention that. I had been thinking the same thing only this morning, and wondering what could be done about it. I know of several small day schools, some of them held only in the morning, but personally I think she's a bit young for that, though one or two of my friends send children who are little more than babies." Frowning, he considered it. "Friends of mine, the Morleys, have a small boy about Julia's age. How would it be if I were to ask Monica Morley to bring him here to tea with you and Julia?"

Verity shook her head. "I'm afraid that wouldn't do. It would put things on the wrong footing, and create a — well, a misleading impression, if I were to act as hostess to a friend of yours. I'm here as Julia's nursery governess, and must behave accordingly."

Barclay's frown deepened. "I suppose you're right, though it's preposterous. And dammed annoying, too! Neither of us would have thought of all these complications, but for that infuriating woman's interference!"

"In that case, I should say it's just as well she interfered!"

"H'm. that's as may be. We must see if we can't think up some way of collecting a few cronies of her own age for Julia.—Tell me, are you fond of music?"

"I love it. Not the modern stuff, though—it's beyond my understanding."

"Good! I'm going to give myself a present. A long-playing gramophone. You'll have to help me over choosing records."

They began discussing various composers, agreeing over Mozart and Beethoven, which they both loved, though Verity found Bach too intellectual for her liking, while Barclay said her favorite Chopin was in his opinion sugary. From music they went on to talk about books, agreeing over one, debating the merits of another, until Ellen's voice announcing dinner took them by surprise, and they realized more than an hour had slipped away.

"Why not have dinner with me, in the dining-room? Then we can thresh out our disagreements over the Whiteoak family!" Barclay suggested.

Smilingly, she shook her head. "No, thank you, Mr. Davenport."

"Why not?"

"For the same reason that I won't play hostess to your friends. I'm here to do a job, and you are my employer, and our two existences are best kept separate."

"Is there so much difference between sharing a meal in the dining-room and chatting by the fire over a glass of sherry?"

"The sherry was unwise. I did refuse it, to begin with. Anyway, two wrongs don't make a right!" said Verity, and left him.

Later, when she had got her tray from Mrs. Bream, and sat alone over her solitary meal, Verity almost regretted that she was not having it with Barclay. It would have been so pleasant to carry on with their discussion, to find more links of mutual interest, to continue making more discoveries about the man who for the most part hid behind a façade of impassive inscrutability.

None the less, she knew she had been wise in her refusal to have dinner with him. If the present situation were to settle comfortably on a permanent footing, their relationship must remain the formal one between employer and employed.

Later that evening Verity unpacked, out of their rustling layers of tissue paper, the clothes that Mrs. Davenport had bought, ready for Jill to wear on her homecoming. She was pierced, as she unfolded them, by poignant memories of how together, they had chosen them so happily.

There was a little black suit, and to wear with it on chilly days a blouse of fine wool patterned in a Paisley design of cyclamen and lime and turquoise. The jacket of the suit was lined with the material of the blouse; it made a charming outfit. There was a little frock of fine black wool, too, pencil slim, and a slender three-quarter length black coat to wear with both the frock and suit. She knew that they would fit her perfectly, for she had tried them on, with many others, so as to give Mrs. Davenport some idea of whether they would suit Jill.

She shrank from the idea of wearing them, these pretty things that she had helped to choose for Julia's mother, but told herself that sentiment helped nobody. One must be practical. Since they were hers, she'd treasure them. It would be nice, she thought, to have something rather special in reserve, for an "occasion !" Then, reflecting that her present way of life held an unvarying uneventful pattern, she decided there would be no point in hoarding them. Better to enjoy them while they were new and up to date !

Next day she was taking Julia to Knightsbridge, to buy new shoes for Julia. Afterwards, they were going—tremendous treat !—to go round Harrods' pet shop. The day was sunny, though Mrs. Bream and Ellen said the wind was cold; it seemed an admirable opportunity for wearing the black suit and coat for the first time. With them, she wore a dashing little hat of soot-black velvet. Mrs. Davenport had finally fallen in love with after Verity had tried on at least a score of other hats for her consideration. Since black, smartest of all for London, looks out of place on most country occasions, this was the first time she had owned a black outfit; she was surprised to find how well it flattered her fair skin, and made her slimness seem more slender still.

Before they set out she looked in on Mrs. Bream, making choux pastry for tonight's savory, tiny puffs filled with creamed haddock. "I'll be at Harrods, Mrs. Bream. Do you want anything?"

"Nothing, thank you. You would be the better of a scarf or something round your neck. You look real smart the way you are, but there's an awful cold wind."

"A scarf or something . . ." Oh, dear! And the only scarf she had was a soft cashmere one checked in brown and fawn, that would look all wrong with her outfit. Serve me right, thought Verity ruefully, for thinking I was elegant for once ! Which shall I be—elegant or frozen? Regretfully she decided to be sensible, and went to get her scarf. Then, as she took it from a drawer, she thought of the baum marten stole, designed to wear with just such a tailored yet sophisticated outfit as the one she wore. She got it out and put it on. The fur lay light and warm about her shoulders, framing her face becomingly in luxurious darkness. If she had looked elegant before, she was a thousand more times so now!

Julia said coaxingly, "Can I go down in the lift all by myself, for a treat?"

She loved to do this, and as it was perfectly safe Verity sometimes allowed it—but not always, otherwise it would soon cease to be a "treat!" Kneeling beside her to make sure her scarf was warmly crossed upon her chest under her coat, she told her "Yes. You may!" and dropped a light kiss on her cheek. Julia said, "Now the other cheek feels left out!"

"We can't have that!" said Verity, and kissed the other cheek.

"And now my *pore* nose is lonely an' niglected!" Julia told her solemnly.

Obligingly Verity bestowed a third kiss on the tip of the neglected nose. "Now don't start telling me your fingers and thumbs and toes are feeling out of it as well, or else we shan't have time to go to Harrods!"

"G for Ground Floor?" said Julia as they approached the lift.

"That's right. I'll race you down!" said Verity, carefully shutting both doors behind the little girl.

She ran downstairs to time her arrival so that Julia would reach the ground floor first, but on the other hand would not have time to struggle with the doors for long enough to work herself into a panic, as once had happened.

As she approached Dr. Gairloch's door, it opened. The psychiatrist herself came out, apparently having a last word with a visitor. In a swift glance at her companion Verity saw that he was a short plump man of about forty. A beaky nose jutted inquisitively from his waxy, egg-shaped face. In his black jacket and dark striped trousers she decided that he looked more like a doctor than a patient—though he might very well be both. Presumably there was no reason why a doctor shouldn't prescribe psycho-analysis for himself!

As she passed them, she bade Dr. Gairloch good morning with an automatic smile. This was the first time they had set eyes on one another since Janice Gairloch had lectured her upon the consequences if she were to stay in charge of Julia, but it could be no surprise to the psychiatrist to see her still here, for she had sent up her housekeeper to spy out the lie of the land under a pretext of borrowing some castor sugar. Mrs. Bream had duly reported the episode to Verity, describing her unwelcome visitor as "A naisty, pasty-faced nosy parker, speirin' this an' speirin' that !"

Verity smiled to herself, remembering Mrs. Bream's account of what had passed.

" 'Ai sewppose the pore little orphaned gel is going tew be sent away tew schewl?' says she. 'Naithin' o' the sort!' says I. 'Mr. Davenport has mair sense than tae send a bairnie little bigger than a babe in arms away from kith an' kin ! The lassie's daein' fine here,' I tell't her, 'wi' her uncle an' Miss Cator tae see after her!' "

Dr. Gairloch returned Verity's greeting by a chilly inclination of her head. If looks could kill, thought Verity as she sped down to the ground floor, the one that's following me now would have the same effect as if she'd thrown a dagger between my shoulder blades. Not that it matters. All the same, it isn't pleasant to be hated . . . She released Julia from the lift. The two of them went hand-in-hand into the cold bright morning, and by the time they reached the end of Harley Street, the trifling episode had faded from her mind.

Dr. Gairloch's visitor was a consultant, Dr. Elvetter, who had dropped in to have a word with her about a patient of his for whom he wanted to arrange a course of treatments with her. Looking after Verity with pale blue gimlet eyes, he said, "Davenport lives above you, doesn't he? I must congratulate him on his taste, next time I see him! Has he acquired a wife without my hearing of it? Or——?" He left the sentence expressively unfinished.

It would have been both natural and easy for her to answer truthfully that Verity had been Mrs. Davenport's housekeeper-companion, and had stayed on after her death to take charge of her little orphaned granddaughter. Instead, she shrugged her shoulders, and with her sneering down-curved smile, told him, "All I can tell you is that Barclay calls the girl his little niece's nursery governess!"

Dr. Elvetter pricked up his ears. He was a bachelor, with a lively tongue that made him greatly in demand at parties. There was nothing he enjoyed more than picking up a morsel of malicious gossip to dine out on.

"Well, well, well!" said he, with an indulgent laugh. "All I can say is that a nursery governess who can afford the furs that girl is wearing must be earning a remarkable lavish salary! And not a sign of any little niece! — Shall I be seeing you this evening at the Prescott's?"

"The Prescotts? Oh, yes, of course — their cheese and wine party. Yes, I shall go if nothing holds me up."

Dr. Elvetter said good-bye and went off chuckling to himself, while Dr. Gairloch returned to her consulting room, well pleased with the turn events had taken. Some kinds of love are close akin to hate. Though she would have married Barclay tomorrow had he asked her, none the less, since he had firmly though politely snubbed her when she had suggested that he was unwise in having Verity in charge of Julia, she had been obsessed with the idea of getting her own back. Jos Elvetter was a notorious gossip. This evening at the Prescott's he would tell the story of the pretty, elegant young woman he had seen emerging from Barclay Davenport's flat — a story that would in no time spread among their circle. Better far that Dr. Elvetter, rather than herself, should be the source of it!

All went as she had hoped. Arriving at the Prescotts' rather late, almost the first person she saw was Dr. Elvetter, the centre of a little group to whom he was vivaciously recounting some amusing tale. She edged her way towards them, near enough to catch a word or two of what he said: " . . . governess . . . most attractive looking damsel . . . "

One of the group, Sir Hartley Dunne, a leading gynaecologist, exclaimed impatiently, "So what?" and turned away, looking annoyed and bored. Somebody laughed, "So Davenport is a dark horse! Who'd have thought it?"

She saw how it would be. Some people would ignore the story. Others, whether they believed it or not, would pass it on. And in a few days it would have grown into a pretty scandal.

An acquaintance in the chattering circle caught her eye. "Dr. Gairloch. What's all this about Barclay Davenport? You're on the spot—you're bound to know all the intriguing details!"

In a few words she might have given a brief explanation of the facts and nipped the gossip in the bud. Instead, she gave her brittle laugh. "Oh, I believe in 'Live and let live.' You'll get no details out of me!" she said, and so, without a word of confirmation, skilfully confirmed the story.

In clubs, at cocktail parties, over bridge and dinner tables, during the next few days the story was repeated with embellishments, until at last, inevitably, Barclay came to hear of it.

He had been operating at St. Michael's. The anaesthetist, a friend of his, said to him as they walked together to their cars, "I say, old boy, I think you ought to know about a tale that's being spread around about you. If it's true, I couldn't care less, and anyway it's no concern of mine. But if it isn't true, you'll want to scotch it right away."

With that, in some embarrassment, he told Barclay that "a raving beauty, dressed from head to foot in mink and diamonds, according to the story going round," was said to share his flat.

When Verity went that evening to fetch Julia to bed, Barclay said abruptly, "As soon as you've got Julia off your hands, I want a word with you."

His voice, and something stormy in his eyes, told her that he had something disagreeable to say. Anxiety made it difficult to hide the impatience she was feeling, when the little girl dawdled over her milk and biscuits.

Free at last, she tossed her apron of bath towelling on a chair, and was about to go to Barclay, still in her white overall, when the nursery door opened and he came in, impatient as herself.

He said, "I've got bad news. Janice Gairloch was right —people are gossiping about us." He told her what his friend the anaesthetist had reported.

Verity felt anger take possession of her, rising like a storm, curiousily exhilarating. "If there is gossip, Dr. Gairloch herself must have started it! Who else would know I'm here?"

"It makes no difference who started it. The point is that I can't allow you to remain in this invidious position. I was wrong to let you stay. It was too much to ask of you.

71

I simply hate to say it—but you'll have to leave as soon as we can make another plan for Julia."

"That's sheer deafeatism! If you think I'm going to leave Julia because of a lot of idiotic tittle-tattle, think again!" cried Verity. "I won't go unless you turn me out by brute force! We've got to fight this thing and beat it —and we will! Now look. I've got a plan. How would it be if you were to ask some of your friends to a small cocktail party? You could pick them carefully—a cross section of the ones you think are likely to have heard this idiotic story. Julia could be with you to begin with. I would come as usual to fetch her, in my overalls. They'd see the set-up for themselves. Surely that would kill the gossip?"

"Surprising how mud sticks, once people begin flinging it around. And this is my responsibility. It isn't fair to you, to let you stay."

She saw how much he hated the idea that she must go. And even if his wish that she should stay were all on Julia's account, none the less it warmed her heart to know that he depended on her.

"At least let's give my plan a chance," she urged him. "Let's not take this lying down. We've got to fight it! Don't waste any time. It needn't be a formal party . . . Why not make a list of people, now, and telephone to them right away?—What are you laughing at?"

"I was remembering the time I interviewed you. I was furious with the agency for sending anyone so young and inexperienced. Little did I dream that all your prunes and prisms concealed a young tycoon!"

She flushed. Was Barclay teasing her? Or had she gone too far? Presumed? She said uncertainly, "I'm sorry! I——"

"Nothing to be sorry for! Quite the contrary! I take off my hat to you. Which variety will you have—billycock— topper—or a smart black Homburg?" He swept off an imaginary hat in a gallant bow, then replaced it.

Relieved, she laughed too. "That's very charming of you. But it would be nice if you would follow up your gallant gesture by doing some telephoning to your friends."

"I will."

"At once?"

"At once!" he promised her. He flicked through the pages of his engagement book. "Saturday seems as good a day as any. That gives five days' notice. I must try to get some people who have children around Julia's age — that might lead to getting her in touch with a few buddies." At the door he paused. "I'm not sure that you're being very wise about this, Verity—from your own angle, anyway. But you're 'a real bonnie fechter' as they say! Good night."

Verity tidied the nursery, which as usual at this hour was strewn with Julia's belongings; folding little garments, laying away toys and books on cupboard shelves. A cherished teddy bear needed repairs; stuffing was bursting from a split seam. She got her mending basket and sat down to deal with it, but did not set to work at once. For some time she sat gazing in the fire and sorting out her thoughts.

She had a strong presentiment that Saturday's party would be a turning point in the affair. No matter how it went, at least the dark cloud of unpleasantness had a silver lining. Until now she hadn't known how much the bond of fighting in a common cause could strengthen friendship, deepen liking.

CHAPTER SEVEN

THE COCKTAIL party was in full swing. To Verity, in the nursery, the noise of talk and laughter drifting along the passage sounded as though eighty people, not a mere eighteen, had accepted Barclay's invitation. She hoped that Julia wasn't feeling lost in such a crowd of strangers.

She need not have been anxious. Julia had been accustomed in Rhodesia to large, gay gatherings. She stayed close to Barclay, smiling shyly, shaking hands with each newcomer, and saying politely "Howjoodo?" Verity had dressed her in a white frock whose scarlet smocking matched her shoes. Her silky black hair curved about her brow and ears in feathery fronds, her long-lashed eyes were starry with excitement, and the guests were charmed with her.

On account of Mrs. Davenport's ill health it had been necessary for her to lead a very quiet life. When Barclay had returned hospitality, it had perforce been in some restaurant. In consequence, although his circle of acquaintances was large, he had been prevented from making intimate frienships save for one or two among the men with whom he worked; the circumstances of his private life were known to very few. So, although most of his guests had heard that he had lost his sister and her husband shortly before Christmas in an air crash, few were aware that they had left a little daughter who was now his ward.

Naturally enough, most of them were members of the medical profession and their wives, including Dr. Gairloch, who as she lived below could scarcely be omitted, and John Girling, the friend who had first warned Barclay of the gossip. Dr. Elvetter, asked although Barclay disliked him for the reason that he was a busybody who had doubtless heard and spread the gossip, had gleefully accepted the invitation in the hope of nosing out the truth about the pretty girl who had flashed past him as he left Dr. Gairloch's flat.

Just as Barclay had hoped, when they saw Julia his guests were full of friendly interest and questions.

Did Julia live here with him? . . . Hadn't it been a great upheaval for him to set up a nursery in his bachelor establishments? . . . Had he found a satisfactory nannie to take charge of her? . . . And so on and so forth, time and again giving him the opening he wanted to make Verity's position clear.

Yes, Julia lived here with him. Where else? Her only other relatives, and his too for that matter, were a few elderly cousins.

No, there had been no trouble in setting up a nursery. In any case, this hadn't been a "bachelor establishment" before her arrival on the scene. His mother had lived with him until her recent death, and very fortunately her companion-housekeeper had stayed on to take charge of Julia and had undertaken the necessary organizing for him. Luckily she was the ideal person for the job—a pleasant girl, and very capable. His mother had been extremely fond of her, the maids liked her, and altogether it had been far simpler and more satisfactory than if he had had to import some stranger.

Meanwhile Verity was screwing herself up to the ordeal of fetching Julia to bed. Dressed as always at this hour, ready for sharing in the splashy business of navigating ducks and fish and boats upon the stormy waters of the bath, she paused beside the open door, momentarily bewildered by the noise of talk and laughter. Really, it was astonishing that eighteen or twenty people could make so much noise!

Barclay was at the far side of the room, his back towards her, talking to a tall, grey-haired woman who looked kind, though autocratic. Julia's small figure was hidden by the taller ones. No doubt she was beside him. Ruefully Verity realized that she must make her way to them among the well-groomed men and chattering women in silly, pretty hats. Still, it was just as well that they should all have ample opportunity of seeing her; after all, that was the object of the party!

There was a sudden lull as first one, then another, saw her white-clad figure as she made her way towards Barclay, murmuring, "I'm so sorry!—Excuse me, please . . ."

Barclay's companion was Lady Dunne, wife of the celebrated gynaecologist. Julia had slipped one small hand into his. She was beginning to be sleepy and a little bored.

Verity said apologetically, Mr. Davenport! I beg your pardon for interrupting you, but I must take Julia to bed. It's after seven o'clock."

"Of course. I didn't realize it was that time." He turned to the tall woman with whom he had been talking. "Lady Dunne, this is Miss Cator, who looks after Julia."

Lady Dunne decided that she liked the candid eyes that smiled so frankly into hers. She liked the girl's expression, too, intelligent, yet kind and gentle. Remembering the gossip passed on to her by Sir Hartley, she felt indignant. Obviously this was a pleasant and thoroughly respectable young woman who was doing a good job under difficult conditions. One only had to see the way the child's face lit up when she appeared, to realize that she was making a success of it. Like as not it was that elegant but peculiar woman Janice Gairloch who had started all the tittle-tattle. Everybody knew she had been chasing Barclay Davenport—without success, as far as one could tell. Dog-in-the-manger tactics would be just like her. Unable to get him for herself, she would be all out to make unpleasantness for any other woman who came within a mile of him. Well—she would lose no time in showing what *she* thought of the situation!

She said, "How do you do, Miss Cator? I have been most interested to meet Julia—she's just about the same age as a small grandson who is staying with us while his parents are enjoying themselves in Switzerland. I am afraid he finds it rather dull, staying with a pair of elderly grandparents. Will you bring Julia to tea with him one day? A very nice French girl looks after him. I think you'd like her."

"Thank you. Julia would enjoy that very much, and so should I," said Verity.

A day and time were settled for the following week. Lady Dunne told Verity, "We live in Lowndes Square. Mr. Davenport will give you the address—you won't remember if I tell you now."

Julia said good night. Lady Dunne, and others too, noted how contentedly she put her hand in Verity's and went happily off with her.

When they had disappeared Lady Dunne, her voice deliberately raised, said, "You were very fortunate in getting such a suitable girl to take charge of Julia, Mr. Davenport! So much happier for a solitary child to be with someone young, rather than an older person—even though her youth has led to complications."

Barclay raised his eyebrows. "Complications?"

"Gossip, my dear man! The most preposterous stories have been going round about the girl, though of course you would be the last person to hear of them. Now that I have seen for myself, I shall take every opportunity of contradicting them."

"Really? What sort of stories?"

"Chiefly to the effect that you are harboring a siren swathed in mink and diamonds, I understand!"

He laughed. "Nothing of the siren about Miss Cator, is there? And have you noticed any mink or diamonds lying around?"

The group around them joined his laughter. Some of them had been at the cocktail party where Dr. Elvetter had first started the rumors. Dr. Gairloch, conscious that they must be remembering that she, who might have nipped the gossip in the bud, had tacitly confirmed it, chimed in.

"All the same, my dear Barclay, it might be advisable to remember the old saying that one should 'avoid the appearance of evil' even where none exists! Miss Cator has some lovely furs, though they may not be mink, and looks as elegant as anybody here, when she goes out."

"Really? I don't know that I've ever seen her dressed for going out. The furs must be the ones left to her by my mother, who as you know was very fond of her. No one with a normal mind could possibly find any 'evil' in her wearing them. I'm glad to hear she does. She was most reluctant to accept them," Barclay answered, then as though the matter were of little interest he dropped it, and turned his attention to the filling up of glasses.

Julia had been in bed for some time before Verity at last heard the welcome sound of the farewells beginning. She had left the nursery door ajar, and clearly heard the cheerful babel made by the departing guests. Evidently they had enjoyed themselves!

Silence told her that the last lingerer must have gone. A moment later she heard Barclay's long, elastic stride coming towards the nursery. He found her ironing a nightdress of Julia's. Other little garments hung to air along the fireguard, somehow looking rather touching and appealing.

He drew a deep breath and exhaled it in a sigh of satisfaction. "M'm! . . . Somehow there's something very innocent about the smell of ironing—particularly when one has been breathing air that's practically solid Chanel No. 5 and cigarette smoke!"

She looked at him with questioning eyes. "Well——?"

"Well . . . It all went off even better than one could have hoped. They all saw for themselves how the land lies." He repeated Lady Dunne's forthright comments, and went on to tell her, "The Gairloch did what she could to spike our guns, but spiked her own instead. I should say there's little doubt that she deliberately started all this nonsense, and that everybody present realized it, and resented it on your account, so that the unpleasantness she meant for you and me has recoiled upon her like a—a——"

"A boomerang!" Verity suggested helpfully. Though it was not particularly funny, out of sheer lightheartedness they laughed.

"So altogether," he went on, "your idea has been a big success, in more ways than one—we've scotched the gossip, and several of the women said they'd telephone and ask you to bring Julia to nursery tea, so it's done her a bit of good as well!" He smiled at her; that sudden charming smile that so transformed him. "All due to you, Miss Cator! How about joining me for dinner, to celebrate our victory?"

Longing to agree, she knew she must refuse. "No thank you, Mr. Davenport. My place is in the nursery, and in the nursery I stay."

"I shouldn't have supposed you to be of a chronically unsociable disposition" Though his voice was quizzical, the smile had left his eyes. She felt as though the sun had gone behind a cloud.

"It isn't that I don't want to have dinner with you!" she protested. "But our 'victory' could so easily become defeat. The enemy is still upon our doorstep. Supposing she—or someone else—has left a bag, or gloves, and came to get them . . ."

"And found us evidently on less formal terms with one another than we gave them to suppose? M'm . . . Yes. We'll have to stay perpetually on our guard. Oh, Lord! And it's all so harmless! But you're right, as usual. You have a way of being right, you know!"

"You sound as though you find it aggravating!"

"Frustrating would express my feelings better. At the moment, anyway!" He stared a moment at the fire in moody silence, then switched to a less personal topic. "Which day are you taking Julia to Lady Dunne's? Tuesday?" He made a note of it in his engagement book. "Hurrell had better take you in the car."

He left her then, abruptly, so that she wondered whether he were annoyed by her refusal to have dinner with him, and in a way regretted it, although she knew she had been wise. But oh, how dreary the wise course could be!

In spite of the successful outcome of the party — or perhaps because of it? — Verity felt depressed, as a chill sense of anti-climax took possession of her. Now that, for a time at any rate, the fight to still the tongues of gossip had been won, she knew that her relationship with Barclay had arrived at a crossroads. Nothing in nature could remain static. Budding friendship either blossomed into deeper intimacy, or withered into nothingness, like a bud that fades and falls before it blooms. She was surprised to realize how great a blank the loss of their would mean in her existence if it should take the second course — as well it might, since henceforth they would lack the link of fighting in a common cause — the bond that in the last few days had done so much to further mutual understanding.

Of late, her thoughts had been entirely focused on the battle to stay on here with Julia. Now, as she took stock of her feelings, she knew that more than Julia was involved. Far more!

She moved the fireguard to a corner of the room, and, turning off the light, sat on the floor as she had loved to do since childhood, one arm on a chair, gazing at the shifting colors of the glowing coals, orange and rose and gold, while spurting flames sent shadows leaping up and down the walls.

Tomorrow I'll be sensible, she told herself. Tomorrow I'll be practical. Tomorrow I'll remind myself that he must know scores of women—girls of his own world, girls with homes where they can entertain him, glamorous girls who move in clouds of heavenly scent that costs about a guinea a drop, and spend as much in beauty parlors in a month as I do on my clothes in a whole year. Tomorrow I'll come down to earth again. But just this once, just for tonight, I'll dream . . .

Her heart leaped at the sound of footsteps in the passage. The door behind her opened. Barclay said, "I flung the drawing-room windows wide to air the room while I was having dinner, and now it's like an icehouse! May I share your fire for what's left of the evening?"

In the confusion of surprise she murmured an inarticulate assent, drawing to one side. Pulling up the second of the two armchairs, he paused. "Has the light bulb died on you? Or are you sitting in the dark from choice?"

"From choice. Besides, it isn't dark, with such a blaze."

Barclay sat down, stretching his long limbs. "My mother used to say that sitting by the firelight did one good."

"Yes . . . I remember once she said that it replenished one's depleted spiritual reservoirs."

"I think it's probably true, in the same way that going out and looking at the stars when one is worried or distressed can put one's troubles in their true perspective."

"Yes—oh, yes! Suddenly one sees what really matters and what is unimportant after all."

"What do you consider 'really matters'?"

She might have felt self-conscious in the revealing brightness of electricity, but firelight helped. "Well—not material things," she said, "though nobody enjoys them more than I do! But their value isn't lasting. Human relationships matter tremendously. To me, at any rate. And the way one looks at life. Evolving a—a kind of personal philosophy. Realizing that when trouble comes, if one accepts it, it can have the same effect as pruning has on roses."

"You're right, of course. You're absolutely right. Twenty-five, aren't you?"

"Yes. But why——?"

"So young to know so much!"

"I think one learns in painful jerks. Life goes on uneventfully for ages, and one doesn't grow. Then some emotional upheaval teaches one a lot."

"But only if one is prepared to learn. So many people aren't."

The firelight dancing up and down the walls gilded their hands and faces as they talked, exploring one another's minds and liking what they found, so much in tune that there was no need for dotting i's and crossing t's, nor even to finish every sentence.

Forgetting time, forgetting everything save the adventure of discovering one another, they talked on till the ringing of the telephone, whose bell was in the passage, broke in with a jarring interruption.

Barclay looked at his watch. "Heavens—getting on for twelve! I should have said we had been talking for no more than half an hour, though it was barely nine when we got down to it! Too bad of me to keep you up so late!—I must go to that wretched telephone. Good night!"

Though she was usually asleep by now, when he had gone Verity made no move to go to bed, but stayed where he had left her, overwhelmed by her emotions.

So this was love! This glorious sense of being perfectly in tune, in complete harmony of understanding, utterly at

81

peace in heart and mind: indescribable, unimaginable until one found it. How could she ever have supposed the restless, turbulent excitement she had known with Euan, heady and disturbing, strangely lonely, like a piece of shoddy, dingy paste in contrast to the sparkle of real diamonds, had been worth the having?

The crossroads she had dreaded had been reached, and safely passed, and in a few short hours left far behind. And now . . . and now . . .

A voice outside called, "Verity? Are you still there?"

"Yes . . .?"

He came in, but remained standing by the door. She rose and faced him, feeling tension in the air.

Barclay said, "You've heard my mother speak of Margaret Duncan?"

"You mean your cousin, who was here before I came?"

"Yes. You know she had to leave because she had to keep house for an uncle, on his wife's death?"

"Your mother told me."

"That telephone call was from her. She rang up to tell me that her uncle died an hour ago. Coronary thrombosis."

"Oh—oh, I'm sorry!"

"So am I. For Margaret. Not for the old man. He was getting on for eighty, and had lost his life's companion. And it was a better way to go than suffering a lingering illness. A frightful shock for Margaret, though. I'd better go to her at Bristol, and cope until the funeral is over. The old man was no relative of mine, but all the same I feel I ought to rally round. Luckily I have nothing on hand that can't be cancelled without any great inconvenience."

"Tomorrow is Sunday," she reminded him.

"So——?"

"Your secretary won't be coming. I was wondering if you'd like me to do some telephoning for you in the morning, to put off your appointments and so on?"

"Thanks for suggesting it. I'll make a list. I want to get off early—it would help a lot." He paused, as though about to tell her something more, then apparently thought better of it. "Well—good night once more!" he said, and went away.

Verity went to bed. Although the radiance of the last hours was as bright as ever in her heart, none the less she felt uneasy, chilled by an indefinable apprehension of she knew not what: a feeling of foreboding, as though some threat were looming. She told herself that it must be the consequence of being tired. The only thing in all the world that mattered now was her relationship with Barclay, and to that his absence for the next few days could make no difference.

Surely she had no reason to be anxious? Surely it was impossible that she should feel this sense of perfect harmony, this unity of heart and mind, unless he felt it too? Surely their budding love would gradually unfold its petals like a rose until the day of blossoming, when they would gather it together? Surely . . . Surely . . . ?

Julia was thrilled when Verity told her they were going to have tea on Tuesday with Lady Dunne's small grandson. During the next two days she spoke of little else.

"What do you think we'll play at? . . . I wonder if he'll have a minicar like mine! . . . Do you aspose the French lady what looks after him can speak to us in English? . . . I *do* hope there won't be egg sangwidges for tea.—You're not *listening* to me, Verity!"

Verity had been wondering what it was that Barclay had thought better of saying to her after he had told her he must go to Bristol. Constantly her thoughts went circling back to that. She had a feeling that whatever it might have been, there lay the clue to the indefinable uneasiness that from time to time possessed her, no matter how much she might reason with herself.

She said remorsefully, "Darling, I'm sorry! If there *are* egg sandwiches, you needn't eat them, so I shouldn't worry."

"Don't I have to eat something of everything for politeness? I usually do when I go out to tea!"

Lady Dunne was out when they arrived, but her grandson Robert, a solemn little fair boy, and the charming French girl who looked after him gave them a warm welcome. No egg sandwiches appeared at tea, to Julia's relief. Afterwards she and Robert built a fort and barracks for his toy soldiers out of wooden bricks. Altogether Julia enjoyed herself enormously.

Verity also spent a pleasant afternoon. The flat was beautifully furnished in an ultra-modern style, interesting and provocative but not at all what she would have expected from the little she had seen of Lady Dunne; this was the first time she had seen anything of the kind. She and Lucienne Devine, with a good deal of laughter and gesticulating, got on well together in halting French and broken English. None the less, as time passed she kept glancing surreptitiously at her watch, wondering whether Barclay, who had said he would be back this evening would have arrived when she and Julia returned to Harley Street.

They were putting on their coats when Lady Dunne appeared, handsome and poised. "Sorry to have seen so little of you. I've been playing bridge—pernicious habit of an afternoon, but someone sent an S.O.S. for me to take the place of somebody with 'flu. Nice that you could come, it's good for Robert to have company of his own age."

"Good for Julia, too. I'm sorry he and Lucienne are leaving you tomorrow—otherwise they might have come to tea with us."

"Another time, perhaps." She looked approvingly at Verity. Sometimes when you'd seen a girl in uniform, you got a shock on meeting her in her own clothes. Not so in this case. The girl looked charming. Perhaps not strictly pretty, but no girl with even white teeth, and a clear skin and those long-lashed eyes, could fail to be attractive! Probably she didn't have a very gay time of it. And young things should enjoy life. She said, "Perhaps you'll come here on your own one evening. Now and then we have a little party for my unmarried daughter's friends. Dancing to the long-playing gramophone, and a fork supper. Nothing elaborate or formal. Would you care to come? Can you get out, when Julia's in bed?"

"I should enjoy it very much indeed. I scarcely ever go out in the evening, but the housemaid would stay on till I get back."

"Good! I'll ring you up one of these days and arrange it."

A week ago, Verity would have been delighted by the prospect of a party, meeting people, widening the vistas of her restricted life. Now, though she was grateful for the kindness shown her, she felt otherwise indifferent. Her thoughts, a blend of doubt and certainty, anxiety and bliss, were all in Harley Street.

When they got back, it was to find that Barclay had not yet returned. A telegram had come to say he would be back tonight, but late, and would have dinner on the train. Verity told Mrs. Bream and Ellen she would make herself an omelet, there was no need for them to stay.

The evening dragged interminably, but at last, after eleven, she heard him arrive. She found him looking through a pile of letters that were waiting for him. Barclay did not hear her, and she stood a moment taking in afresh the details she already knew by heart: the dark head set well on broad flat shoulders, the determination of the thrusting jawline seen in profile, above all the shapely hands, so strong and yet so sensitive.

His sombre face lit up as he looked up and saw her. "Hullo! What are you doing, up at this hour? I imagined you'd be sound asleep!"

"I though you might like something hot, after your journey. Soup, perhaps? Or coffee?"

"Nice of you! No, thanks. I don't want anything." She would have said good night and left him to his letters, but he stopped her. "I'm afraid I have a piece of rather tiresome news. You'd better hear it right away. I won't delay you long. Come to the fire. — My cousin, Margaret Duncan, wants to return here. I was afraid of this before I left, but felt there wasn't any point in mentioning what after all was no more than a possibility."

"To return here? Do you mean — to take my place?"

"That was her suggestion, yes. I told her right away there could be no question of it. But I can't refuse to let her stay here, for a time at any rate, while she is making plans to readjust her life. She can't stay on for more than a few days in her uncle's house; the executors naturally want to clear it out and sell as soon as possible. She has nowhere else to go but here. My mother's room is empty, and she knows it."

"Oh, but of course! Poor soul—it must have been such a dreadful shock to her . . ." Thankful that the "tiresome news" was nothing worse than this, Verity was already mentally choosing books to put beside Miss Duncan's bed, arranging flowers to stand upon her dressing table Barclay's grim expression puzzled her. Why should he mind so much? Was Miss Duncan a tremendous chatterer? Would she disturb him of an evening when he came back tired, wanting to read in peace?

She asked, "What is Miss Duncan like?"

"Like'? We-ll—she's forty-ish. Brisk and bright. Capable. Confident. Managing. Knows all the answers." He paused to light a cigarette, then as he clicked the lighter shut and slid it in his pocket, he said, "But the real trouble is this—she's hand in glove with Janice Gairloch!"

CHAPTER EIGHT

VERITY, AS SHE walked up Harley Street with Julia from their morning walk a few days later, reflected rather ruefully that for some time to come she would need all the tact at her command. This very afternoon Miss Duncan was arriving, and the situation during her visit was obviously going to present difficulties. For Verity herself it would be far from easy not to feel that she was being constantly if silently criticized by the older woman who had organized the household here before she came. And for Miss Duncan it might well be something of an effort to refrain from commenting on this and that, and to keep what by all accounts was a most efficient finger out of the pie that was no longer hers.

Miss Duncan's friendship with Dr. Gairloch was another factor to be reckoned with, for the psychiatrist was sure to try to stir up trouble between Barclay's cousin and the girl whose presence in his home she so resented.

Anyway, she thought, I'll do my utmost to make her visit go off happily. Though she does sound rather terrifying, Mrs. Davenport must have been fond of her, and they were cousins, so there must be something nice about her!

On the way back from the Park they had visited a flower shop where she had bought freesias for the visitor's bedroom, and daffodils, blue irises, and rosy tulips for a mixed vase in the drawing-room. Before going out she had put the vases ready in position, filled with water. There would be ample time to arrange the flowers before Miss Duncan came, and to put the final touches in her room, as she had written to Barclay that she would be arriving about four o'clock.

"When we've had lunch," she said to Julia, "before you have your rest you can help me to choose books to put in

Cousin Margaret's bedroom. And we'll fill the biscuit tin beside her bed, as well."

However, they had no sooner reached the second floor than they were pounced upon by Mrs. Bream, who had evidently been looking out for them.

"She's come!" hissed Mrs. Bream in a conspiratorial whisper, her wide red face redder than ever from agitation.

"Who's come?" demanded Julia in her piping treble.

"Wheesht, dearie!" Laying a dramatic finger on her lips, Mrs. Bream drew them into the kitchen and shut the door behind them, then announced, "Miss Duncan's here. She took an earlier train — she's brought six cases and two baskets and a parcel and a hatbox. Ellen was giving the drawing-room a good turn out and half the things were in the passage when she got here. If it had been yesterday, when we were having mince, it wouldn't have been so bad — you can always put in another carrot or two. But nobody can turn four grilled soles into five, not with the best will in the world, and though I 'phoned the fish shop right away they say they can't send round in time."

"Perhaps there'll be a miracle!" Julia suggested hopefully.

"Don't you worry, Mrs. Bream," said Verity soothingly. "I'll have bread and cheese. I like it every bit as much as fish." She hoped she didn't look as dismayed as she was feeling. What a beginning! Empty vases. Not a sign of welcome. Oh, dear . . . !

"We'll take our things off, darling, and I'll tidy you before we go and speak to Cousin Margaret," she said to Julia. Ellen was laying lunch for one, clattering the silver crossly, as they passed the open door of the dining-room. "This is a nice to-do!" she grumbled. "Miss Duncan surely could have let us know that she was coming earlier, instead of catching me in such a muddle as you never saw!"

More soothing. "I know it's very trying for you, Ellen. But we must remember poor Miss Duncan is recovering from a nasty shock."

"No worse than the shock *I* had when my stepgrandmother choked upon a kipper bone half-way through her

88

tea and never took another mouthful, not in this world. But I hope it didn't make *me* inconsiderate to others!" Ellen sniffed.

Verity said that she was sure it hadn't, and how nice the silver looked, and escaped. Five minutes later, leading by one small clinging hand a Julia whose dark hair gleamed like silk from careful brushing, she went with smiling lips and inward nervousness to greet the new arrival.

They found Miss Duncan sitting by the fire, surrounded by a quantity of her belongings. At her elbow stood a workbag slung on folding legs. Against her chair was propped a large embroidery frame on which was a half-finished chair seat — or perhaps a firescreen? — in a conventional design of mauves and blues with touches of maroon, on a grey background. By her feet lay an open attaché case, and she was writing something on a pad upon her knee.

Verity remembered Barclay had said that she was "forty-ish" and thought it was an apt description; probably she had looked forty for the last ten years and would continue to look forty for another ten to come. Her face was broad, her features neat, her coloring nondescript, with sandy brows and lashes, pale eyes, and a faded skin. Her head was rather large, and set upon a short neck; her hair, which in her youth had probably been curly, now looked dry and wiry and had faded to a grizzled mouse-color. She wore a plain grey tailored suit, an uninteresting white silk blouse, and sensible black shoes.

She looked up from the letter she was writing as Verity and Julia came in. Fighting with shyness, Verity said, "Good morning! My name is Verity Cator. I'm a sort of mixture of housekeeper and nursery governess! I am so sorry not to have been here when you arrived, but Mr. Davenport said you would be coming about four o'clock. It all seems so unwelcoming — no flowers in your room, or here . . ."

"No welcome necessary, thanks! I'm very much at home here, I assure you! —So this is Julia?" Her ungracious manner became bluff and hearty. Margaret Duncan didn't care for children. She was full of theories concerning them, but in their presence became self-conscious and uneasy, and her uneasiness made them uneasy too, without quite knowing why.

Julia hung back against Verity, who gave her a gentle little push. Shyly she went forward, holding out a hand politely.

"Howjoodo?"

Miss Duncan took the small hand in a large plump freckled one, and shook it heartily, up and down and up and down repeatedly, making a joke of it, so that Julia felt her gesture had been silly in some way she couldn't understand; it was what she had been brought up to do.

"How d'you do — how d'you do — how *do* you do!" said Margaret Duncan facetiously. "How old are we?"

Doubtful as to whom she meant by "we" Julia looked back uncertainly at Verity, who came to the rescue. "Julia will be four next month."

"H'm! Not a very big girl for four, are we? Quite a midget! We shall have to see if a nice big bottle of cod-liver oil will make us nice and tall. And what a pity that she hasn't got her mother's pretty curls. That wispy hair, so straight and fine, is always difficult and unbecoming." She spoke as though Julia were a doll, incapable of understanding.

Verity changed the subject hastily. "Will it disturb you if I arrange the flowers here now? They 'stay put' so much better if one does them on the spot. I would have done them sooner if I'd known that you were coming by an earlier train."

Miss Duncan said that she would do the flowers herself. But not in that white vase. Bring me the blue bowl from the pantry — unless you've broken it? I always use it in this room. It looks so charming with the chintzes."

With mutiny in her heart, Verity brought the bowl. It certainly looked quite well with the chintzes, but the shade of blue clashed with the irises, which with the yellow daffodils and rosy tulips would have looked far better in the white china vase she had prepared for them.

"I got some freesias for your bedroom. I'm so sorry they weren't there to welcome you. Would you prefer to arrange those, too, or shall I do them?"

"Freesias? Oh no, thanks! Scented flowers are so un-healthy in a bedroom. Still, as you've got them. I can use them with the others." Later in the day Verity found the poor little freesias, their delicate pastel flowers lost among Miss Duncan's stiff arrangement of the larger, brighter blooms.

Tears began to slide down Julia's face as they went back together to the nursery. "That lady said I were a midget!"

"Darling, she only meant that you aren't very tall. And that's nothing to mind about. There's a saying, 'Good things are made up in little bundles'!" said Verity con-solingly.

Julia shook her head vigorously. "No, she didn't mean that! She meant that I'm the same as one of those little ugly tiny *horrid* people on the television when we went to tea with Robert!"

Verity had much ado to comfort her.

Lunch time was approaching when she realized she had forgotten to give Miss Duncan Barclay's message of apol-ogy that as he had a busy day he would not be returning before six o'clock or even later. As she approached the open door of the drawing-room she heard Miss Duncan speaking on the telephone.

"That you, Janice? Margaret here! Yes — I knew you'd be surprised! Poor Uncle Henry died last week. I'm back for good . . ." (*For good?*) "Yes . . . Yes, that would be delightful, thank you! About half-past five? Right. You must tell me how the land lies!"

She replaced the receiver. Verity went in and gave the message, feeling considerably shaken by what she had over-heard.

She had believed, and so had Barclay, that Miss Duncan's visit was to last only until such time as she could make some more permanent arrangement for her future. Now it seemed that she intended to take up her abode here for good! It would be difficult for Barclay, in that case, to get rid of her without unpleasantness. And unamiable though she had been to start with, she would certainly be far more so after hearing Dr. Gairloch's verdict upon Julia's nursery governess!

"Come in, my dear! This is a wonderful surprise!" said Janice Gairloch, trying to sound more enthusiastic than she felt, and marvelling for perhaps the fiftieth time that the cousin of a woman with such charm as Mrs. Davenport could be so unprepossessing as Margaret Duncan. Only her usefulness as a stepping stone into the household overhead had caused her to make overtures of friendship to this boring woman who was so frumpish, so opinionated, so provincial mentally as well as physically.

"Come and sit down and tell me about everything," she said, thinking how incongruous Margaret's drab, dumpy figure appeared against the sophisticated background of her ivory and celadon and lilac room. She would have been scornfully amused could she have known that Margaret was thinking what a mistake poor Janice made in liking to have everything so bare. It would have improved the room so much, she thought, to have some little tables here and there, with a few knick-knacks such as paper knives and photographs in silver frames, and snuff boxes and carved ivories. And that really was a *most* peculiar picture all triangles and zigzags! A few nice water colors in gilt frames, of bluebell woods and highland cattle on magenta moors, would be a great improvement. But then these brainy women seldom had good taste. Even her clothes were queer, though there was no denying they were elegant. Some colored beads, or a nice artificial posy, would have cheered up that dress of hers, and if she must wear green, a nice bright jade or emerald would have been more interesting than that wishy-washy shade she was so fond of.

They sat down together, Janice elegantly poised, Margaret with skirt tucked up, feet planted wide apart. "Now tell me all about yourself!" said Janice. To her dismay, Margaret took her literally. Only the psychiatrist's professional training and experience enabled her to hide her growing irritation and impatience, as with a wealth of tedious detail Margaret poured out the tale of Uncle Henry's sudden death, her own reactions, the inconsiderate behavior of the daily help, the tiresomeness of the executors, until at last she managed to interpolate, "Actually, it's just as well that the executors wanted you to leave. High time that somebody responsible should take charge up there!" She pointed to the ceiling.

Margaret blinked her sandy lashes. "What . . . ? Why . . . ? How . . . ? You mean . . . ?"

"I mean, my dear, that the young woman in whom Barclay has put so much misplaced confidence needs putting in her place — and keeping there!"

"I *thought* as much! I meant to ask you your opinion of her. She takes too much on herself — apologizing for having been out when I arrived—regretting having seemed unwelcoming — as though I needed any welcome from a stranger into what is virtually my own home! And yet poor Mary seemed to think the world of her, judging by letters."

"Oh, she did! The girl took care of that! In no time she had Mrs. Davenport twisted round her little finger. I did drop a hint or two, but it was like water off a duck's back."

"Mary was always far too sweet and kind for her own good. But I should have thought Barclay would have seen through her."

"My dear Margaret, does any man ever see through a woman who sets out to make herself attractive to him?"

"Make herself——" But surely—you don't mean——?"

"But I do 'mean'! From the beginning she has set her cap at him. If something doesn't happen soon to put a stop to it, that girl will be Mrs. Barclay Davenport."

Margaret Duncan was aghast. She had been cherishing a cosy mental picture of herself, snugly and permanently established in the luxury of Barclay's flat, to all intents and purposes its mistress. Somehow the possibility that he might marry had not occurred to her. She was accustomed to regard him as a bachelor, absorbed in his career, and imagination was a quality she lacked. Janice, as she saw anger succeed dismay in her small pale eyes, was well pleased with the effect of her words.

Margaret jerked out, "But it would be most unsuitable! Barclay ought to marry — if he marries at all, and he's quite happy as he is — someone with a title. Or at the very least a girl of social standing!"

"All I can say is that he will probably marry an impecunious little nobody, unless something puts a stop to it."

"Something shall — *I'll* see to *that!*" declared Miss Duncan energetically. "How providential that I was able to come back in the very nick of time!" Blinking her pale eyes, pursing her small prim mouth, she began considering how to set about it.

Janice Gairloch, watching her speculatively through the smoke she was exhaling from her chiselled nostrils, could read the workings of her mind, and realized that they might be the better for a little guidance. "There is only one solution — to get rid of her. And that may be more difficult than you suppose. The girl has character. Obviously she will put up a fight to stay where she has hopes of catching an extremely eligible husband."

"I could make things so unpleasant for her that she might be glad enough to go."

She's such a blunderbuss that she'll make a nonsense of it if I don't put on the brakes a bit, reflected Dr. Gairloch. She said, "You'd have to do it without letting Barclay realize what you were up to. Still, he's out a great deal. That should help."

An unwelcome thought made Margaret pucker up her brows. "If she were to leave, I should have Julia on my hands."

"Julia could attend a kindergarten. And you could get a nursery housemaid to look after her, instead of Ellen."

"I never *did* like Ellen . . ." She sat pondering for a moment, then rose briskly, looking purposeful. "What a mercy you were on the spot, to put me wise to this! Otherwise I mightn't have suspected it for quite a time.— I must be off. I shall pop down now and then to let you know how things are going. And you will come up and see me, won't you, when you have a spare moment?"

"I will indeed! And you must let me know if I can help in any way. Two heads are better than one."

Janice smiled her curious down-curving smile when she had closed the door behind Miss Duncan. The seeds of trouble she had sown for Verity had rooted swiftly, and in

94

fertile soil. It would be interesting to watch them grow —
as speedily, she hoped, as Jack's beanstalk!

Verity was reading *Jemima Puddleduck* to Julia when
Barclay put his head round the nursery door. "I gather
Margaret has arrived, from her belongings littering the
drawing-room, but there's no sign of her. Any idea what's
happened to her?"

"I think she's probably gone down to see Dr. Gairloch,"
Verity told him. Julia rushed to clasp him round the
knees. "She said I were a midget! I don't *like* her!"

Over her head Barclay asked, "Everything all right?"

He looked more tired than Verity had ever seen him.
She knew he had been doing a difficult operation during
the afternoon whose outcome had been worrying him. She
hoped the patient had not died. This was obviously not
the moment for telling him that it seemed Miss Duncan
meant to stay here permanently. She smiled at him more
cheerfully than she was feeling. "Perfectly all right!"

"Good! I wish I could say the same, I've had a hell of
a day." He swung Julia up into his arms. "Come on, old
lady! I'm a bit late, but there's time enough to build a
few card houses before bedtime."

Verity could hear Julia persisting in the passage, "But
I *aren't* a midget, am I?" And his reassuring answer, "Of
course you aren't. You're just exactly right!"

No matter how unpleasant and difficult Miss Duncan
may make things for me, I shan't tell him unless it becomes
quite impossible to carry on, she decided. He has enough
upon his shoulders without having to worry about petty
trivialities as well, if I can keep them from him.

"Soup!" said Miss Duncan. "It's the first time I remember having it beneath this roof. Times have changed!"
Her words were harmless, yet her manner managed to
imply that this minor innovation was a major disloyalty
to Mrs. Davenport.

"It didn't suit my mother. That was why we never had
it," Barclay told her. "I like beginning dinner with it."

Miss Duncan made no comment, but decided that as
soon as she took over the housekeeping, soup should be

cut out, for it was fattening, and she gained weight all too easily.

"I was most upset not to be with you when you so badly needed someone of your own, while you were going through that dreadful time of sorrow just before Christmas," she remarked, altering her reproachful note to a condoling one.

The last thing Barclay wanted was to discuss with her those days of tragedy. He made a noncommittal sound, and asked if she had had a comfortable journey.

"Quite, thank you. And now I *am* here, I must make up for lost time and start getting things in order right away."

Barclay raised his eyebrows. "I am unaware of any particular disorder, I must say!"

Miss Duncan changed her tone again to one of soothing tolerance, as she observed that men didn't notice things about the house as women did. "I have no doubt Miss Cator manages little Julia very well, but one can't expect a girl like that to manage in the same way as a woman of experience. Not that there's much wrong that I can't put right very soon. I will go into everything tomorrow morning."

"Thanks very much, Margaret. But I'm perfectly satisfied with the way Miss Cator runs things, and as you have come here only until such time as you are able to make permanent arrangements for yourself, it would only serve to create confusion if you were to interfere. I hope while you're in London you'll amuse yourself — get in touch with friends and see some plays, and so on."

Miss Duncan knew from past experience that arguing with Barclay never got one very far. She told herself that if she simply stayed on here and made no plans to go, he would gradually take her presence in the flat for granted, as before. Meanwhile, without his being aware of it she could make things so unpleasant for That Girl that she would leave. Barclay would be glad enough when that time came to have his cousin on the spot, to take the reins!

She said, in a bright artificial voice, "Have you read anything good lately?"

Verity had folded up her sewing and was about to go to bed when her heart leapt at the sound of Barclay's footsteps in the passage, followed by his voice. "May I come in?"

Oh, lovely bonus of delight! She had supposed that she would see no more of him this evening.

He said, "I was afraid you might have gone to bed. I snatched the chance to have a word with you while Margaret is telephoning. — Look, I'm afraid we may be in for difficulties."

"We" — enchanting word when it meant "You and I" — and "I" was Barclay!

He went on, "Margaret spoke at dinner as though she thinks I'm going to have her here for keeps. Talked about taking over the housekeeping, and so on."

"I suppose it's natural for her to regard this as her home. Your mother was so kind. She probably encouraged her to feel that about it."

"Yes. Yes, that's the crux of it — my mother's attitude towards her. Margaret is one of the most irritating females it has ever been my lot to meet. Even in this short time I daresay you've discovered how infuriating she can be! But Mother saw her with compassion, while I only see her with exasperation. Mother remembered her as an unhappy little girl, cursed with an unattractive personality, and, because of it, unpopular with other children — sensitive enough to be aware of that unpopularity, yet too obtuse to realize that being bossy and interfering didn't help . . . trying to ingratiate herself with the grown-ups by telling tales, and failing there as well. Because of that pathetic background, my mother managed to feel only pity and loving-kindness for her, though most women in the same position would have found her irritating beyond words."

"How typical of Mrs. Davenport!" Verity murmured.

"Yes, wasn't it? So you see, I must do what I can to let her down gently. I did tell her that you'll carry on with running things, when she suggested taking over. And I spoke of this arrangement being temporary. But more than that I can't do! I *can't* lay down a date when she must go. Not yet, anyway . . . I only hope that you won't find her too insufferable — that she won't make things difficult for you. If she does, you'll have to tell me."

Verity wished he didn't look so tired and troubled; wished, too, that she could protect him from this trivial yet annoying addition to the greater burdens he must bear connected with his work: the daily problems he must face of human suffering and life and death.

"Oh, don't you worry about that! It's not as though I shall be seeing much of her," she assured him.

"Mrs. Bream and Ellen don't much care for her, I fancy, though they put up with her for my mother's sake. You may have a spot of bother there."

"I'll be on the lookout. Forewarned is forearmed!"

He smiled at her, that sudden, charming smile of his. "I feel much better, now I've got that off my chest! — I must get back to Margaret. Good night!"

When he had gone, Verity with some surprise discovered herself almost hoping that Miss Duncan would be thoroughly unpleasant to her in the days ahead. I'd positively enjoy having something to endure for Barry's sake! she thought. Then, laughing at herself, she went to bed.

Margaret Duncan had finished her telephoning a few minutes earlier. Where had Barclay disappeared to, all this time? Opening the door a crack, she listened. Presently along the passage a door opened, and she heard him say "Good night!"

So he had been with That Girl — had slipped away to snatch a word with her at the first opportunity!

Janice had been right. She must get rid of her as soon as possible, before something came of it.

Barclay found his cousin busy with her embroidery frame. Her placid face gave no clue to the spiteful plans she was evolving in her head.

CHAPTER NINE

THE MORNING AFTER Miss Duncan's arrival, Verity went to look for her, and found her stitching at her chair seat, by the fire. The floor around her feet was strewn with wools, books, magazines, a writing pad and envelopes. It looked as though she meant to spend the morning indoors.

Verity said, "Good morning! I do hope you had a good night, and were comfortable?"

Miss Duncan raised her sandy brows, as though surprised at this concern about the welfare of one so very much on her own ground. "I slept as well as usual, and was quite comfortable, thanks."

"I'm on my way now to arrange about the meals with Mrs. Bream. I wondered if there's anything in the way of food that you dislike? Or specially enjoy?"

Miss Duncan answered curtly that Mrs. Bream was well aware of all her tastes.

Verity ignored the snub. "Shall I ask Ellen to bring you something at eleven? Tea? Or coffee? Or do you prefer Ovaltine or something of that sort?"

"Ellen knows very well what I like."

"Yes, but I'm afraid she won't do anything about it unless I tell her, as it's I who give the orders. So if there's anything you want, do ask me. Mr. Davenport is very anxious for you to be comfortable, and he will be most annoyed with me if I don't see that you have all you want."

"Thanks. Mr. Davenport knows very well that I'm quite capable of taking care of myself!"

Verity said no more. In silence she made up the fire, then left Miss Duncan to her stitching. As she shut the door she pulled a rueful grimace. Of all the disagreeable, ungracious creatures! But I won't let her goad me into being as unpleasant as she is herself. There's nothing that would give her greater satisfaction than telling an exaggerated tale of my misdeeds to Barclay.

Her difficulties were not ended. Mrs. Bream showed signs of being on the verge of one of her moods, and Verity had to use all her tact and spend a considerable time in soothing her back into a good humor. However, at last the meals were written in the menu book, the order list made out, the necessary telephoning done, and she set off with Julia for their morning walk.

Returning sometime later, they were met by Ellen with a face of thunder. "You were no sooner gone than the bell rang and she said she wanted a cup of some drink she called Yuveema at eleven."

"Oh, *dear!* I've never heard of it — and I *did* ask her if there was anything she wanted!" Verity lamented. "What did you do about it?"

"Telephoned the grocer's, but they couldn't send it in time. And nothing else would suit! I took her coffee and biscuits — that was what she always had when she was here before. But no! My lady gave the tray I brought her such a look you might have thought that it was poison I was offering her, and curled her lip as though the place was going to rack and ruin. If you ask *me*, I think myself that she was dying to have the coffee—it was just to be as aggravating as she could that she refused it! So I drank it up myself rather than waste it. And very nice it was."

"Have you ordered some of this Yuveema?"

Ellen said she had. It would be here this afternoon. "The grocer says it's something newly on the market. I don't doubt that she was longing for her coffee, and only asked me for this other stuff to put us in the wrong, because she knew we wouldn't have it. Well—from now on she shall have it every morning of her life, and I just hope she'll take a scunner at it, as Mrs. Bream would say!"

Annoying though it was, Verity told herself it didn't really matter, and with an effort put the petty episode from her mind. However, something far more trying was to follow later in the day. As she was settling Julia for her rest when they had finished lunch, Ellen appeared. "Miss Duncan wants to speak to you, when you're free."

She found Miss Duncan still at her embroidery frame, as though she had not left it since this morning. Verity said, "Ellen tells me that you want to speak to me."

Miss Duncan bent her head to peer at her above the pink rims of her spectacles. "Yes," she said, "Yes, I do indeed!" Slowly and with deliberation she took off her spectacles and put them in their case. To fill an awkward silence Verity said pleasantly, "I'm so sorry the drink you wanted for elevenses wasn't available—if only you had told me you would like it, when I asked, I would have got it for you from the grocer's myself. It will be there for you to-morrow."

Miss Duncan paid no heed to her apology. Propping her embroidery frame against her chair, she placed her fingertips together in a judicial manner, and said, "I understand that it was you who went through Mrs. Davenport's belongings on her death?"

"Yes. Mr. Davenport asked if I would see to it. It was at my suggestion that he sent you her enamel toilet set, and various other things. Not knowing you, it wasn't easy for me to guess what you would like. I do hope you were pleased with what I chose?"

Miss Duncan did not say whether she had been pleased or not. She said, "My cousin had some pieces of good jewellery. What became of them?"

So she had coveted the diamond clip, the string of pearls, the ruby ring, the diamond one, the jewelled wrist watch, and the pretty, sparkling earrings!

"Mr. Davenport has put it for safe keeping in the bank, until Julia is old enough to have it."

"*All* of it?" probed the inquisitor.

"Why not ask him?" Verity suggested.

"Who listed it?"

"As it was already listed for insurance purposes, a new list was unnecessary." (*Really*—! Is she implying that I helped myself to bits and pieces while I did the sorting out?)

"And what became of Mrs. Staverley's belongings? Were they all lost in that dreadful accident?"

"Not all of them. I disposed of what was salvaged, for Mr. Davenport."

"How?"

"In various ways that I — and Mr. Davenport — considered suitable."

"Was there any jewellery?" She stared at Verity suspiciously, as though suspecting her of wearing poor Jill Staverley's pearls hidden beneath her dress, her diamond clip behind its lapel.

"Miss Duncan, it would really be more satisfactory for you to ask Mr. Davenport anything you want to know. I'm only his employee." (I *won't* let this insufferable woman make me lose my temper!)

"Precisely! That is why I so regret not having been able to leave my uncle and take charge here when the — the tragedies occurred. It is really terrible to think of all my cousin's belongings being disposed of by a stranger without any supervision — any check——"

Any *check* — as though I were a thief! Verity turned upon her heel and left the room, with a great effort closing the door quietly — she longed to vent her feelings by a hearty slam.

I've got to try to make allowances, she told herself. I've got to try to see her as the unhappy little girl she used to be, unpopular and bossy and pathetic. I've got to try to realize how disagreeable and trying I might be myself, if I had that behind me. I've got to pity her, instead of letting her enrage me! Otherwise the situation will become intolerable. Above all, I mustn't let Barclay suspect how difficult she's being, or he may explode. And if he does, we'll all of us regret it when it's too late.

So when Barclay came that evening to the nursery to fetch Julia for her hour with him, and asked, "Everything all right?" Verity smiled, and gave a reassuring answer.

The next few days were filled with petty irritations, each one trivial in itself, yet adding into an exasperating total. Verity avoided Miss Duncan as far as possible, but it seemed as though the visitor lay in wait to pounce on her at every opportunity. Each encounter left her ruffled, all the more so since she was angry with herself for minding.

The visitor's requests were endless, and her comments,

harmless on the face of them, somehow invariably concealed a barb.

Would Miss Cator tell Ellen that she liked her nightdress *laid* on her hot bottle—not wrapped round it? And that she preferred a variety of biscuits in the tin beside her bed—not just one sort? Would Miss Cator remind Mrs. Bream she liked her breakfast egg boiled for five minutes and a half *exactly*, neither more nor less? And also that she liked her cutlets very well done? At dinner last night she had had one that was positively pink inside . . . What silver polish were they using now? . . . Oh. Perhaps that explained the difference she had noticed. *She* had always seen to it that "Glit" was used, with excellent results . . . Had Miss Cator noticed that Ellen had become very careless in the way she used the Hoover? There were several new marks on the skirting in the passage. "Of course, if *I* were keeping house, I'd speak to her myself about it. But one realizes that for you it may be difficult. Although a woman of that sort will accept reproof from a member of the family, from a girl in your position it's a very different affair!"

Fortunately her sense of humour, applied to an improbable mental picture of Ellen meekly listening to Miss Duncan's dignified rebuke, helped Verity to keep her temper.

Never did Margaret Duncan set eyes on Julia without t't-t'ting disapprovingly, before remarking that she would be boiled today in such a thick coat, or frozen without a scarf, or that a dark frock would be more suitable for a little girl who lived in London than a skirt and jersey, which were meant for country wear, or that if Julia were in *her* care she would make her rest before lunch instead of after, and so on and so forth until Julia was bewildered and Verity thoroughly on edge.

However, it was not difficult to keep the state of things from Barclay, as owing to Miss Duncan's presence in the flat she seldom saw him now save briefly, or in his cousin's hearing, so that confidences were impossible. In one way this was perhaps as well. Yet, lacking the reassurance of their former constant contact, Verity at times found herself wondering whether after all that sense of perfect, blissful harmony between them, lighting all her days, making her feel as though the sun were always shining in her heart, was born of her own longing, and existed only in her imagination, felt on her side, but not his. Her mood veered constantly, from happiness to depression, certainty to doubt. If only — oh, if *only* Miss Duncan would make some plan for a permanent future, pack, and go, so th᷉ life here might return to its former ways! Only when that happened could she see the slightest chance of Barclay and herself resuming the relationship that had been brought abruptly to a standstill by the intrusion of his cousin in their lives. But of her departure there was no sign, and sometimes Verity felt she would be here forever, growing daily more exasperating.

Miss Duncan went down constantly to the first floor to report developments, or rather lack of them, to Dr. Gairloch. "That Girl must have a skin as thick as a rhinoceros!" she declared. "No matter how much I may hint the place is badly run, and criticize, she simply smiles and turns a deaf ear."

"What about Barclay? Have you dropped a few hints there?"

"I did, in the beginning. But I had to stop. He didn't take it well. The very smallest criticism, and he was on the defensive right away."

The fact was that Miss Duncan found it very difficult indeed to discover any flaw in the way Verity ran the household. When she herself was doing it, she had been handicapped by the dislike of Mrs. Bream and Ellen, who for the sake of Mrs. Davenport had put up with her, but none the less detested her for her patronizing, overbearing manner and continual fault-finding. Therefore all that they had done for her had been done grudgingly. When she had suggested Mrs. Bream should try out some new recipe, always there had been difficulties and objections, so that in Miss Duncan's day there had been little variation in the meals. When, to Ellen, she had suggested some improvement—that the silver candelabra might be brought out from their green baize wrappings in the cupboard and used now and then upon the dinner table in place of the glass candlesticks, or the Georgian sugar dredger used from time to time instead of the crystal sugar bowl, Ellen had declared that she had enough to do already without cleaning extra silver.

But with Verity it was another matter. Tactful, friendly, unassuming, always generous with praise where praise was due, she was well liked by both Mrs. Bream and Ellen. With her, they did not feel that she was giving orders, but requesting their co-operation, working with them as a team. In consequence, they gave her of their best. Secretly, although she made no comment, Miss Duncan was annoyed to see the candelabra and sugar sifter whose appearance on the table she had often but in vain demanded were now in constant use, while the improvement in the food was quite surprising. The meals were varied and imaginative. Mrs. Bream, stimulated by Verity's encouragement and interest, was for ever hunting out new recipes, with appetizing results which Barclay obviously appreciated, to the chagrin of his cousin. Her own enjoyment of the delicious fare was blighted by her feeling that to take a second helping would be playing into the enemy's hands; she had a hearty appetite as well as being greedy, so it was pain and grief to her to shake her head, with ostentatiously curling lip, when Ellen handed her some tempting dish—a sacrifice for which the hope that her contempt for Verity's imaginative catering would be reported in due course to That Girl, was poor recompense.

Dr. Gairloch was impatient over what she regarded as Margaret's spineless attitude. "I suppose you did suggest to Barclay that you should take on the housekeeping?" she asked. "That would put you in a much stronger position."

"I suggested it the very first night I was here! It didn't work. He took the line that it would only make confusion in the long run, as he seemed to think I would be leaving soon. I had to drop it in a hurry and talk of something else, for fear he might pursue the subject and begin discussing possibilities for my future plans."

"Has he talked of anything like that?"

"Not yet, and I am hoping that if matters drift, he never

will. I'm tempted now to let things take their course, and see what happens."

" 'What happens' will be that the Cator girl will catch him, if you leave her in possession! Really you must make an effort to get rid of her. If you do, he'll obviously have to let you stay to run things for him. But if she marries him, first thing she'll do as the new Mrs. Davenport will be to put you out upon your ear. Surely between us we can think up something that will really get beneath her skin and make her leave!"

Miss Duncan, unaware that this concern was all in aid of getting rid of Verity, and that once this had been achieved Janice Gairloch would take no further interest in Margaret Duncan and her future, told her it was very nice of her to try to help. However, for the moment they could think of no drastic way of ousting Verity.

For two days more Miss Duncan kept up her campaign of petty irritations, vainly hoping for results: That Girl appeared serenely unperturbed, no matter how much she might carp.

And then, one evening, matters reached a climax. Ellen's niece was going to be married. Naturally Ellen was going to the wedding. Mrs. Bream had been invited too. Afterwards there was to be a party of the family and friends, lasting all the evening. Mrs. Bream told Verity of this, adding that she would stay as long as possible, but would get back in time to deal with dinner; she could do most of the preparing in the morning.

Verity refused to hear of it. "Of course you mustn't miss a moment of the party, Mrs. Bream! As it happens, Mr. Davenport is going out that evening. I can easily serve Miss Duncan's dinner—soup and a grilled sole and a sweet omelet, or something of that sort."

As luck would have it, on the morning of the wedding day, Miss Duncan got to hear of it, and straight away went down to Dr. Gairloch, who was preparing to go out and was not best pleased to see her. On hearing what Miss Duncan had to tell, she mellowed.

Five minutes later Margaret Duncan, on returning to the top floor, told Verity, "Oh, Miss Cator, Dr. Gairloch will be dining with me tonight, to keep me company as Mr. Davenport is going out."

Verity opened her mouth, shut it again, drew a deep breath, and said with her most pleasant expression, "Would you like dinner at the usual time? It makes no difference at all if you would like to alter it."

First blood to me, this round! she thought. It would have enchanted her to see me look put out, and even more so if I'd said that it was inconvenient—she could have reported that to Barclay.

Miss Duncan, looking blank at meeting no objection to the news that Verity would have to cook and serve dinner for a guest as well as for herself, said that the usual time would do.

Verity said nothing of the altered plan to Mrs. Bream and Ellen, knowing that it would take some of the gilt off their gingerbread if they were to know that she would have to do more work on their behalf than had originally been planned. She waited until they had gone, Ellen resplendent in a blue dress and a fox fur, Mrs. Bream in brown, her rosy face redder than ever from excitement, before she laid the table with an extra place and altered what was already laid. I'm going to do them proud! she told herself: I'm going to pile their plates with coals of fire!

Julia had had a good walk in the morning, so after she had had a rest they went no farther than Marylebone High Street, to do some shopping for this evening's dinner. Then, while Julia settled down to have a doll's tea party in a corner of the nursery, Verity set to work.

At Bleydon she had picked up a good deal of kitchen lore by watching Hannah, and had enjoyed cooking the evening meal for Aunt Laura and herself when Hannah could be coaxed not to leave some dish prepared so that she need do no more than warm it up. But since she came here, she had had little practice in cooking, since Ellen enjoyed doing it on Mrs. Bream's half-day. To begin with she felt slow and clumsy, and was handicapped by being unfamiliar with the contents of the cupboards, so that she had to search for everything she wanted. However, gradually she settled down and felt at home.

She had decided that the first course should be the sole she had meant to grill for Miss Duncan's main course, filleted, the fillets curled round chopped anchovies, dotted with dabs of butter, cooked slowly in the oven, and covered at the last minute with a creamy cheese sauce. This should be followed by veal cutlets in a casserole, with mushrooms, olives, tomatoes, and a *bouquet garni* to be removed before serving, of thyme, a bay leaf, parsley stalks, and a sprig of rosemary. And the meal should end with a cold sweet she had learned from Hannah, who called it mimosa fluff. This was made of egg yolks beaten together with sugar and lemon juice, slowly cooked in a double saucepan over boiling water until they thickened to a cream, then folded into the stiffly beaten egg whites. Piling the pale gold foam in a glass dish, Verity slid it into the refrigerator, while Julia, armed with a teaspoon, blissfully cleaned out the bowl.

Barclay came in late that evening; there was no time for his hour with Julia. He had to change and go off in a hurry to his dinner, to his cousin's relief. She had said nothing to him of her expected guest, and had felt increasingly uneasy as the day wore on as to his reactions when he learned of what she was imposing on Verity. She had a vague idea that this dinner he was attending was some official function. It was sure to go on fairly late; Janice was certain to have gone when he returned. With any luck he'd never know that she had been here, and by tomorrow, like as not, he'd have forgotten Verity had been deputizing for Mrs. Bream and Ellen.

As soon as Julia was safely tucked away in bed, Verity took a tray with drinks and glasses to the drawing-room, and was glad to find it empty, so that she could make up the fire, straighten cushions, and put all in order without a critical eye upon her. From the kitchen, presently she heard Miss Duncan greet Dr. Gairloch effusively on her arrival. Fifteen minutes should be long enough for them to have their drinks, she thought, so at the end of that time she announced, correctly as a well-trained parlormaid, "Dinner is served!"

Miss Duncan gave her a brief nod, but made no move and the two women went on talking. Verity realized that nothing would please them better than to put her in the wrong by ruining the dinner. Luckily the casserole would come to no harm, but she was concerned about the fish. It wouldn't be her fault if it were spoilt, and yet, illogically, she would feel to blame. Hoping for the best, she put in the warming drawer below the oven, and when ten minutes later Miss Duncan and her guest at last went to the dining-room, no harm had been done; it looked delicious, with the cheese sauce delicately browned on top.

With the casserole of veal she handed creamed potatoes, beaten to a fluff with butter and hot milk and lightly sprinkled with chopped parsley. As she was about to leave the room, Miss Duncan called her back. "Miss Cator! Is there no second vegetable?"

"There are mushrooms and tomatoes in the casserole," said Verity with flaming cheeks.

"Oh, dear—well, if that's all you'd better hand it to us again. We should have taken more if we had realized.— I do apologize, my dear!" she said to Janice Gairloch, "though I did warn you it would only be a scratch meal!" *Scratch meal—!* She wins that round! But anyhow I won't give her the satisfaction of seeing that I mind.

Presently as she handed the mimosa fluff, she asked, "Would you like coffee here, or by the fire?"

"By the fire, as usual.—No small knife and fork? Are we to have no savoury?"

No savoury—as if three courses weren't enough, and more than might have been expected, in the circumstances! "I'm giving you a savoury that doesn't need a knife and fork," she answered quietly.

Back in the kitchen, she sprinkled parmesan cheese thickly on ice wafers, added a suspicion of cayenne, and having toasted them beneath the grill, produced the savoury and felt that she had won the final round.

She served the coffee, hot and black and strong, then went to do the washing up, thankful that the ordeal had been brought to a successful ending. But she had been too optimistic! Barely had she turned on the hot tap when the drawing-room bell rang loud and long, as though an impatient finger had been pressed upon it and held there in annoyance — or perhaps determination to annoy?

Taking a deep breath, holding her head high, she went to face whatever was in store now. As she reached the drawing-room, Dr. Gairloch was speaking in her carrying, metallic voice. Her profile was turned towards the door; out of the corner of her eye she must have seen that Verity was there, but she went on talking as though she and Miss Duncan were alone. "My dear Margaret, what does it matter? Don't apologize! One can't expect a girl of that type, lacking any background, to know how things should be done!"

Miss Duncan had the grace to look embarrassed, but she had been egged on to make herself unpleasant, and to draw back now would bring upon herself a scathing tirade from Janice. Secretly, she was beginning to be a little nervous of Janice, with her bitter tongue and overbearing ways!

She said, "Miss Cator, you forgot to sweep the hearth and make the fire up when we were in the dining-room! Kindly do so now."

"How *terribly* remiss of me!" said Verity, not troubling to disguise the sarcasm in her voice. The hearth was tidy save for one small piece of cinder that had fallen from the fire. She swept it up. The fire was burning well and should have lasted for another hour or two without addition, but she piled on more coal, unpleasantly aware of the two unfriendly pairs of eyes watching her every movement, and thankful that her hands were steady.

"Empty the ashtrays," said Miss Duncan when she had finished, "and fold the evening paper. And the tray of drinks should have been removed while we were having dinner. Nothing looks more squalid than used glasses! Take them away. And you had better come at ten to see what we should like then in the way of nightcaps. Meanwhile, bring some logs — this fire wants cheering up — you've nearly put it out!"

The mutiny in her heart nearly boiled over into angry words. With a tremendous effort Verity swallowed them, feeling as though they would choke her, and left the room carrying the tray — then nearly dropped it in astonishment at finding herself face to face with Barclay, who was standing in the passage by the open door. His cousin had been mistaken in supposing him to be at some official function; he had been dining with a man who had to leave to catch a night plane for America, and so had returned early.

Barclay laid a finger on his lips and shut the door behind her, took the tray, and motioned her to go ahead of him. Not until he had put the tray upon the kitchen table did he speak.

"What the devil's going on here?" he exploded.

Verity explained, wondering how much he had overheard.

"D'you mean to tell me Margaret deliberately asked Janice up to dinner, knowing you would have to cook for them?"

Verity said nothing.

"Why in the name of fortune didn't you tell her she could go to blazes and get a meal herself? — Tell me, does she often speak to you as offensively as she was speaking now?" Not waiting for her answer, he went on, "We've got to thresh this out, but I must go down now to the consulting room to do some urgent telephoning — otherwise the man I want a word with may not be available. Let's see ——" he took out his engagement book, riffling through its pages. "When you've settled Julia tomorrow for her rest, join me in my consulting room. I'm clear till three, and we can talk there undisturbed, which isn't possible up here with Margaret snooping round. Obviously the whole set-up must be reorganized as soon as possible. Meanwhile, I'm more sorry than I can say for having let you in for this! — I must go, or I'll miss this chap I want to speak to. Good night!"

He was gone. Verity washed up mechanically, scarcely knowing what she did. All her exasperation of the last hour was forgotten in this new suspense.

"Obviously the whole set-up must be reorganized as soon as possible . . . reorganized as soon as possible . . ." Through her mind the words echoed and re-echoed time and again. ". . . reorganize as soon as possible . . ."

Yes — but how? What changes waited, hidden round tomorrow's corner?

CHAPTER TEN

FOR SOME REASON Verity would have found it hard to analyse, she was reluctant for anyone to know that she was going to have a talk with Barclay in his consulting room. She put on an outdoor coat, and took her bag and gloves to give the impression that she was going out, before asking Ellen to keep an eye on Julia as she rested, "just in case she calls for something that she wants — it only happens once in a blue moon! I will be back long before it's time for her to get up."

To her surprise, as she met Miss Duncan in the passage on her way to the stairs, that lady made some comment on the weather, reinforced by the stretching of her small pursed mouth into a wintry smile.

Verity was astonished by this unusual condescension, wondering what could have caused it. The fact was, that Miss Duncan was uneasy over her behaviour of last night. She knew that, goaded on by Janice Gairloch, she had gone too far, and wondered whether That Girl had told tales to Barclay? Whatever the reason, his manner at breakfast had been frigid. All very well for Janice to keep urging me to make things difficult for Miss Cator — it's myself, not Janice, who will suffer if there are unpleasant repercussions, she thought resentfully. It's me, and not the Cator girl, who may have to leave a haven where I live in luxury at no cost to myself, unless I'm careful how I play my cards!

Evidently mere unpleasantness wasn't going to work. For a few days she would hold her hand and see what happened.

To Verity's relief, Dr. Gairloch's door remained shut as she passed it, going quietly downstairs. The tall house was unusually silent, for the lunch hour was not yet over; no muted tapping of the secretary's typewriter sounded from behind her closed door. Mary Pridham was absent

112

from her post of duty in the hall, no bell rang to announce arrival of some patient; there was no sound save the distant murmur of the traffic and the thudding of her heartbeats as she paused a moment on the lowest step, one hand resting on the banister.

She was remembering how often she had come running down these selfsame stairs so as to meet Julia at the lift after she had come proudly down alone and quickly slide the door open before the little girl had struggled with it vainly, with mounting panic; remembering how happily they had set out together for their walks, or come back with a laden shopping basket or a sheaf of flowers, how every time she crossed the hall she had glanced at the door of the consulting room with quickening heart, wondering whether it would open, and Barclay would emerge, or whether she would hear his calm deep voice, speeding some parting patient. And she was wondering, tortured by uncertainty, whether all these little, ordinary, happy things had happened for the last time — whether Barclay had decided that to end a situation which had become impossible, Julia should go to school, his cousin run the household as before, and she herself forever leave all that had come to mean so much: the house that she had learned to look upon as home, the child she dearly loved, and above all the man who was the centre of her dreams and hopes, the root and core of her existence . . .

The door of the consulting room was ajar, and evidently Barclay had been listening for her, for as she approached she heard the movement of a chair hastily pushed back, followed by his swift elastic stride across the room.

He flung the door wide. Neither spoke. As he drew back for her to pass their eyes met, but for all her passionate anxiety, in his she could read nothing of his purpose. Darkly inscrutable, they searched her own until she lowered them, afraid of what they might betray.

This was the first time she had been in his consulting room since that October afternoon when first she came here, and they had taken stock of one another across his desk. How much had happened in the five short months that had gone by since then! During that time she had known deep content and met with enmity. Happiness had been swiftly followed by the shock of cruel tragedy. Julia's clinging arms had taught her a new tenderness, and she had found strength out of her desire to help. And through it all had been entwined the thread of her relationship with Barclay, steadily but surely changing from antagonism to respect, to liking, now at last to love, as though a thread woven in a tapestry had gradually brightened from a dark ugly shade to dazzling gold.

Barclay said, "Won't you sit down?"

Obediently she took the chair where she had sat during that first daunting interview between them. Barclay, as before, faced her across his wide, flat desk. How many times, she thought, he must have played his part in scenes of human drama within these four walls! How often, seated where he sat now, he must have known the pain of breaking tragic news, the happiness of ending the cruel torture of suspense with a reassuring verdict!

Glancing at her coat and gloves, he raised his brows. "You're remarkably well wrapped up, surely, for a journey from the top floor to the ground?"

"I wanted — anyone who saw me — to suppose that I was going out."

He frowned, so that his dark face grew darker still. "Things must have reached a pretty pass if you're afraid of having a perfectly normal action misconstrued! I'd no idea, until last night, that Margaret was being so offensive. Obtuse of me. The last week has been pretty gruelling and I'm afraid I've had my mind on other things than her behaviour. Has that sort of thing gone on the whole time she's been here?"

"Never quite so badly as last night. I daresay she was worse because of having Dr. Gairloch there, backing her up."

"Egging her on would be more like it . . . So she's tiresome as a general rule?"

"She's never very easy to get on with," Verity admitted, "partly, I think, because she's jealous of my having dealt with all your mother's personal belongings . . ."

He uttered an impatient ejaculation.

"Also, she must hate my being here. She must regard

me as an obstacle that prevents her from returning permanently."

Barclay was silent. He had taken up a pencil, and was twirling it this way and that. Fascinated, Verity watched the unconscious dexterity of his fingers. He said at last, "How about Julia? Is all this nonsense having any effect on her? Do you think she feels a certain tension in the air? Or does it pass above her head without her being aware of it?"

"I'm afraid she *is* aware of — well, of an uneasy atmosphere. She is included in it."

"*Julia* is? How do you mean?"

"Oh, I don't mean that Miss Duncan scolds her, only that she makes Julia the channel for a lot of criticism aimed at me."

"How d'you mean?" he asked again.

"Always there's something wrong, every time Miss Duncan sets eyes on her! She shouldn't be wearing that thick coat on such a mild day. Wouldn't it be a good idea to have her hair cut short? If that were done, it mightn't look so unkempt and wispy. Brown shoes are unsuitable for little girls in London — they look too countrified. Fancy a big girl of nearly five still wearing mitts instead of proper gloves! No one would think to look at her that she had plenty of good plain food and lots of milk — she's such a skinny little scrap! So pasty, too — does she have plenty of fresh air? Is her window open wide at night? . . . Always something! I don't think Julia exactly minds, but it bewilders her. And it's beginning to make her so self-conscious." Unhappily she ended, "Oh, I didn't want you to be bothered with all this!"

He said impatiently, "I told you that you were to tell me if things became difficult. Yet you would have kept this to yourself, if I hadn't turned up last night at a crucial moment?"

"Of course! It's all so trivial!"

"I don't agree. Perpetual pinpricks can become intolerable. Their cumulative effect may do more damage, in the long run, than some major catastrophe. It's got to stop."

So he was going to say that Margaret Duncan must leave. Thankfulness leapt in her like a flame, then died down as she knew she couldn't let him do it.

Barclay went on, "Verity, I——"

She interrupted him. "Things may improve. I met her on my way down, and she was almost friendly — smiled, and made some remark about the weather. Don't — please don't tell her she must go! No one to turn to — nowhere to go — to leave would be disaster for her!"

"My dear girl, I——"

"Your mother managed to feel pity and loving-kindness for her. We must do the same—picture her as the unhappy child she used to be, and make allowances. That's what your mother did. That's what she would have wanted us to do."

"Look, Verity——"

"Oh, I do wish I hadn't said so much! If she has to go, I'll feel I've made you turn her out. I——"

Barclay leaned across his desk towards her. "*Will* you kindly let me get a word in edgeways?"

Abashed, she said in a small, defeated voice, "I'm sorry!" and was silent.

"What *is* all this outburst?" he demanded. "Have I said a single word to the effect that Margaret must go?"

Mutely, feeling foolish, she shook her head.

The irritation left his face. "Sorry for storming at you!" he apologized. The atmosphere returned to normal.

Verity laughed. "Sorry for babbling at you!" she retaliated.

Barclay said, "What I was going to suggest was something of a very different nature. Something I'd been meaning to postpone for quite a while, until I felt the time was ripe. But this has forced my hand." His eyes were on her face, intent and searching, as he asked, "Verity, would you consider marrying me?"

For a long moment she was speechless from sheer astonishment, while his dark eyes held her own as though by some magnetic force that flowed between them. When her voice returned it was a husky whisper. "*Marrying—!*"

Quickly, reassuringly, he said, "Oh, not yet! Not until you have had ample time to get used to the idea of it.

And to me! But meanwhile, it would make the position considerably easier for you if we were engaged."

Verity was wordless, waiting. He went on, "As my future wife, you would have a completely different standing. Even Margaret wouldn't dare to play up any longer. She would take good care to mind her p's and q's, knowing how greatly I should resent anything in the least unpleasant in her behaviour towards you." He paused a moment, before adding, "And there would be an end to the anxiety over Julia."

She tore her eyes away from his and stared down blindly at her hands, gripped together in her lap. Later, with surprise, she was to find red marks where her nails had pressed into her flesh, but now she did not feel the pain of it.

Oh, bitter sweet! The moment she had dreamed of, longed for in her secret heart, had come at last, and brought instead of bliss this unspeakable pang of piercing pain. The moment that should have brought their flower of love into the full perfection of its blooming . . . the flower that after all had no scent, no more sweetness than a plastic rose, and tore her with its hidden thorns.

Magic words that should have been spoken in a firelit room, scented with burning wood, or in the moonlight sweetness of a summer garden, had been uttered in a room walled with books on medical lore, over a business desk: uttered with no sign of tenderness, no word of love, no hint that anything save expediency was involved. For him, a permanent solution to the problem of Julia's upbringing in the happiest of circumstances. For herself, security, a home, position.

Then had it, after all, been only wishful thinking on her part to believe he shared her feeling that they were, so to speak, tuned in on the same wavelength, perfectly in harmony, on the threshold of a deepening relationship, vital to both of them? Barclay had said of his proposal that it was "something I'd been meaning to postpone for quite a while, until I felt the time was ripe. But this has forced my hand." At least, then, it was no sudden impulse. But it was all so puzzling!

117

What did it all mean? What was she to say to him? To Verity, the passing seconds seemed like hours, while she was struggling with bewilderment, lost in the confusion of conflicting thoughts. Barclay must like her. That was one crumb of comfort: he must like her very much indeed, to have considered asking her to be his wife, to share his life. And yet, if she were to agree to be engaged to him, would mere liking be enough to hold him in a bond that should be based on love? Mightn't the fact of being engaged to her gradually change that liking into an irritable feeling of being fettered, ending any possibility that might grow to match her love for him?

She could not know that echoing over and over again in Barclay's mind, as they had echoed many a time in the past weeks, were his mother's words, spoken after she had told him of Verity's unhappy love affair.

"When a woman has been badly hurt by one man, her reaction nine times out of ten is to distrust and fear all men for some considerable time. With Verity, it has gone very deep indeed, poor child. So deep that I'm afraid it will be many a long day before her attitude to men and love and marriage is restored to normal."

Seeing the indecision on her downcast face, he bitterly regretted having let his hand be forced, before the time was ripe, by the uncomfortable conditions brought about for Verity by Margaret Duncan. He'd been a fool to risk it. . . .

Verity said, her voice sounding in her own ears strangely distant and detached, "You've done me a tremendous honor in suggesting this—paid me the very greatest compliment possible. I do realize that, and — and appreciate it more than I can say. But I'm afraid . . . I'm very doubtful as to whether liking is a—a strong enough foundation for such a very vital and important thing as marriage!"

He had known she liked him, but to hear her say so was extraordinarily pleasant. Yet if he were too persistent, made her feel that she was being hustled, liking might be changed to the "distrust and fear" his mother had foretold. He must go carefully. It was evident that to try to force the issue now could only be disastrous.

So Barclay took her words as a refusal, without argument or persuasion. He said, "I'm sorry. But if that's how you feel, there's no more to be said. Try to forget it happened, if you can! On my side, this will make no difference."

"Nor on mine, of course!" she told him quickly.

"Now, about Margaret—I'd better talk to her this evening like a Dutch uncle. Tell her that if she doesn't mend her ways, she'll have to go."

"Couldn't you leave it for a few days? She's been different today. Actually quite civil, when I met her in the passage on my way down! I have a feeling that she knows she went too far last night, and is uneasy. I think it might be just as well to see how far she goes on, before you say anything."

"Right. I'll hold my hand meanwhile. But only on condition that you tell me right away if she goes on making a nuisance of herself. Promise?"

"I promise!" she agreed, and rose.

No more was said by either of them. Barclay reached the door before her. As she passed him she was sharply conscious of his closeness, of his broad, hard shoulder on a level with her cheek, of his slight characteristic odor, blended of shaving cream and Turkish cigarettes and a faint hint of some disinfectant. For a moment she was seized by poignant longing to be taken in his arms, to feel them tightening until she was his prisoner, to lift her lips to his, ardently responsive to his demanding tenderness.

The moment passed. The door had closed behind her, and she was alone again—no, not alone, for as she crossed the hall towards the lift, Mary Pridham's surprised voice behind her exclaimed, "Why—Verity! I'd no idea that anyone was with His Lordship! Have you turned patient?"

She forced herself to laugh and answer lightly that she hadn't been consulting Mr. Davenport about her health—they'd been discussing a domestic matter.

Upstairs, luck was with her. Julia, who seldom dozed during the afternoon rest, was sound asleep, so there was time to think, alone and undistracted, before she need take up the threads of every day. She sat on a low chair, chin cupped in her hands, staring in the nursery fire, and going over in her mind all that had just passed between herself and Barclay.

It was wonderful to know he liked her well enough to pay her the supreme compliment of asking her to be his wife. Otherwise, no matter how expedient, nor what the motive, he had far too much sense to take such a momentous step. . . . And yet—and yet, he had immediately construed her words of doubt into a definite refusal, not attempting to persuade her to see matters in a different light, expressing no hope that she might change her mind, and only a perfunctory regret. . . . She wonderer whether his proposal had been made for Julia's sake, or whether, owing to some new outbreak of gossip, he had felt compelled to make it out of chivalry.

She began to wonder whether Barclay, seeing her so often, living under the same roof for months, had become too accustomed to her; whether familiarity had created unawareness of her as a personality? Were that so his liking, grown of habit, might have reached its limits.

And she thought—perhaps he's got too used to having me around, running his home, part of the background of his life like Mrs. Bream and Ellen and his secretary. Oh, if only I could make him see me in a new light! *See* me, instead of taking me for granted! Yes—but how?

Her speculating had a speedy answer. As she went to see if Julia were waking, Ellen came to tell her she was wanted on the telephone.

A voice said in her ear, "Katherine Dunne speaking!"

Katherine—? Oh, of course—Lady Dunne. How long it seemed since Verity had taken Julia to tea in Lowndes Square with her small grandson! Time was very odd. Ten days could seem eternity, or seem to concertina into a fraction of the time.

Lady Dunne went on, "We are having a small impromptu party tomorrow evening. Nothing formal—dancing, and a fork supper, for my daughter and her friends. We shall be very glad if you can come, although the notice is so short."

"Thank you so much for asking me—I'd love to come! How kind of you!"

"Splendid! Nine o'clock tomorrow evening. I look forward to seeing you!"

Lady Dunne rang off.

Nine o'clock! Oh, heavens! That meant the party would go on till twelve, or even one. She couldn't possibly ask Ellen or Mary Pridham to stay as late as that, and yet it would be so disappointing to have to leave while all the fun was still in full swing.

As she was standing by the telephone, wondering what to do, Miss Duncan came in, looking so much less disagreeable than usual that on a sudden impulse Verity explained what had happened. "So I wondered, if you won't be going out tomorrow evening, if you would very kindly leave your bedroom door ajar, so that if Julia's is open too, you'd hear her if she woke and called? She never does, but all the same one couldn't risk leaving her with no one within earshot."

Margaret Duncan's first impulse was to say ungraciously that she wasn't here to act as nursemaid. But remembering Barclay's frigid attitude at breakfast, she decided to go warily until her position here was more secure, so she answered affably enough that she would do as Verity suggested. So that was settled. She could go without a qualm on Julia's account . . . Julia, who by now was wide awake, and clamouring to get up.

"I'm going to a party!" Verity told her. Julia was much intrigued. What sort of party? Would they play games? Would there be a conjuror? Would there be jellies? And crackers?

Verity was not thinking that she would enjoy the party, but that her wish would be fulfilled: Barclay would see her for the first time in another aspect, going out, wearing an attractive frock, to join in gaieties to which he had not been invited.

When Julia had been tucked cosily in bed the following evening, Mrs. Bream appeared as Verity was tidying the nursery. She was carrying a tray. On it, on a pale blue plate, lay a delicious looking omelet, palest golden brown, its filling of mushrooms oozing from its edges.

"Now just you eat this up! Oh, yes—I ken fine you'll begetting supper at your party! But that won't be before

121

ten, or mebbe later. You'll be famished long or that time, if you don't get something now."

Verity felt that she would never want to eat again, but Mrs. Bream stood over her commandingly to make sure she did as she was told. The kindness of it warmed her heart, and when she had begun to eat she was surprised to find that she was hungry. Keyed up emotionally, she had eaten very little since her interview with Barclay yesterday. When every morsel had been eaten, Mrs. Bream went off, well pleased, with the empty plate, and Verity began her preparations for the party.

First a bath, relaxed at leisure, lapped deliciously by water scented with bath oil. Silken underwear she had been treasuring for some special occasion, palest peach, with ecru lace. Foundation cream, powder carefully applied with cottonwool, a trace of vaseline on brows and lashes, grooming them to glossiness with a tiny brush, a touch of lipstick, softest rose. . . . Her face was ready!

Last night she had washed her hair. She brushed it now until it gleamed like satin, sweeping back in soft loose waves of palest brown from brow and temples, curving round her neck and ears to frame her face becomingly.

Some time before Christmas she had bought an evening frock, egged on by Mrs. Davenport one day when they were shopping for Jill—poor Jill, who had never seen her mother's presents. . . . "There will be gaieties at Christmas, so you're sure to need it. And it's so becoming that it might have been specially made for you!" Mrs. Davenport had told her.

The frock had been a model, and the original cost would have been far beyond her means, but a pair of scissors dropped points downwards in the skirt had made a tiny tear, bringing the price down to a bargain that she could afford. The tear, which she had mended skilfully, was now invisible, lost in the full folds of the chiffon. It was in a gentle shade of hyacinth blue. The softly draped crossover bodice was caught at the waist on one side by a velvet rose; the skirt was very full, a bell of misty blue over a stiffened petticoat.

Tying a square of chiffon lightly over her face and hair, Verity dived into the dress, emerging like a swimmer from a wave. The blue drifts settled gently into place, flattering her creamy arms and shoulders, deepening her eyes, floating out about her as she moved, romantic as a distant waltz heard in a moonlit garden on a summer's night— the *Merry Widow, Bitter Sweet,* the *Blue Danube.* . . . Oh, it was even lovelier and more becoming than she had remembered!

From its bed of rustling tissue paper she took out the sable cape Barclay had intended for his mother. The furs embraced her in a light caress, luxurious and soft and warm. A last glance in her mirror showed a girl with starry eyes, a girl who looked as though she had no care in the world and who had never done a day's work in her life, a girl who might have been the cherished daughter of a millionaire.

Yet it would all be wasted, useless, unless Barclay saw her and became aware of her in a new light, as a girl who could be glamorous as well as practical, frivolous and gay as well as workaday. With all her might she willed him to come out into the passage as she left her room.

Either her "willing" worked, or fate was kind, for as she approached the drawing-room door it opened. They were face to face. Longing to see him startled into a new awareness of her, hopeful that his eyes would light with admiration or at least with interest, disappointment chilled her when at the sight of her he did not move a muscle of his dark, impassive face. For all he cares, she thought forlornly, I might just as well be wearing my white overall, or a skirt and twin set. . . .

"Going out?" he asked.

She felt like answering, "Oh, no—I just thought it would be fun to dress up in a party frock and ride up and down in the lift until it's time to go to bed!" Hiding her exasperation, she explained where she was going, and that Miss Duncan had kindly agreed to keep an ear open for Julia.

"I'll come down with you and get a taxi."

"Thank you, but there's no need—I ordered one for five to nine."

"I'll come down all the same and see you into it." He moved towards the lift.

"I'd rather walk," she said. She couldn't bear to think of being with him in the lift, intolerably near, intolerably far apart.

"As you like!"

In silence, side by side, they walked down. As he open-the front door, the taxi she had ordered drew up. Barclay made as if to put a hand beneath her elbow to help her in, but withdrew it without touching her. "Good night. Have a good time!" he said, and slammed the door.

Sick at heart, she leaned back in a corner with closed eyes, hating the idea of going to the party. All very well for him to say what happened yesterday between us would make no difference to him! she thought. Nothing can ever be the same again. The atmosphere between us is completely changed.

Desolately she wondered whether her refusal had hurt him? Angered him? Was liking lost, and friendship spoilt?

The taxi stopped. She had arrived.

As she stood upon the pavement in a pool of light from a street lamp, counting out the coins to pay the driver, a second taxi drew up. A man got out. A voice behind her exclaimed, "Good Lord! *Verity!*"

Turning, she was face to face with Euan.

CHAPTER ELEVEN

EUAN STARED incredulously at the girl he had last seen far away in Norfolk, on an autumn afternoon. Then she had been a country girl, in tweeds and sturdy shoes, ingenuous and unsophisticated, smiling up at him with love-lit eyes. The same girl faced him now: the same, and yet how different!

This new Verity had poise. She looked a million dollars! She was beautifully groomed. Expensively, as well—those sables must have cost a packet. But the chief change was in her eyes, whose first surprise at seeing him had changed to cool appraisal. No love for him shone there now. She looked at him as though he were a stranger, and an uninteresting one at that.

"How amazing—meeting you like this!" said Euan jerkily, jolted from his normal self-possession by some thing disconcerting in her expression, something baffling. Mockery? Amusement? He couldn't quite make out.

"Amazing? Why? Lowndes Square isn't private property." She drew her furs about her. "It's too cold to stand talking here!" she said over her shoulder, as she turned towards the entrance to the block of flats. As he started after her, his taxi driver called " 'Ere. 'ere! Wot about my fare?"

Cursing inwardly at having made a fool of himself at this particularly ill-timed moment, Euan paid the man and hurried after Verity. He caught up with her as she was opening the door of the lift, which had just descended. "Are you going to the Dunnes', by any chance?" he asked her, as he joined her in the lift.

"Yes." She did not ask "Are you?" She did not even look at him. Opening her evening bag, she began examining its contents as though to see if something she might want had been forgotten. Dammit—the girl might be a little more responsive! After all, it wasn't long ago that she had liked him well enough to be prepared to marry him! Yet now, for all the pleasure she displayed at meeting him again, he might have been the dustman!

Euan would have been still more piqued could he have known all that was passing in her mind; that she was wondering how she could ever have believed that this fair, good-looking stranger with the calculating eyes and selfish mouth meant everything in life to her—thankful that he no longer had the slightest power to move her.

A smiling Austrian maid was waiting to admit guests to the first-floor flat, where earlier arrivals were already dancing; sounds of music and gay voices came from an open door. The maid showed Verity to a bedroom, then returned to her post of duty. Having laid her furs upon a bed already strewn with coats and wraps, Verity lingered at the mirror, giving small unnecessary touches to her hair, hoping that if she loitered long enough Euan would be dancing with some other girl when she emerged. However, when she left the bedroom he was in the hall, making polite small talk with Lady Dunne, whose smile at Verity was warmly welcoming.

"So nice to see you!"

Verity smiled back. "So nice of you to ask me!"

The girl looked really charming, thought her hostess. Probably she didn't know a soul here. One must remember to look after her and see she had a good time. Meanwhile, it was fortunate that Captain Gilmerton was at hand as a beginning. Lady Dunne did not greatly care for him; it was her daughter who had invited him. He was too suave for her liking, always too ready with the right remark, the well-turned compliment. She had summed him up as insincere, with too much of an eye to the main chance. Still, at a party he was undeniably an asset, good-looking, entertaining, and an admirable dancer. She lost no time in introducing him to Verity, and was considerably surprised when Euan smilingly explained that they were old friends. "We hail from the same Norfolk village!"

Verity, her face expressionless, said nothing.

"Shall we dance?" Euan asked her.

"Thank you." She would have liked to snub him, liked to make it plain that she had long since recovered from her one-time infatuation for him, but with Lady Dunne beside her there was nothing for it but to agree.

Lady Dunne looked after them as they went off together, thinking what a good-looking pair they made. She hoped that nice girl shared her own opinion of the handsome Guards officer. Young people nowadays were apt to take a hail-fellow-well-met attitude towards one another, very different from the more formal and certainly more romantic relationships that had existed in her own young days. Yet Lady Dunne suspected that behind the brave facade the modern girl presented to the world, of casual companionship, unsentimental camaraderie, many a one was every bit as vulnerable to heartbreak as those of her own generation. And a man of Captain Gilmerton's type, lacking imagination, and with no thought save for himself, could cause cruel hurt to such a girl. When this dance ended she must see to it that the Cator child met nice John Saunders, and Hugh Naunton, and the Gillespie boy. Euan took Verity in experienced arms. So short a time ago (yet in some ways it seemed a lifetime!) his touch had thrilled her. Now she felt no more emotion than if she were dancing for the first time with some uninteresting stranger.

"Fabulous frock that is you're wearing!" Euan told her.

"Think so?"

"Prettiest in the room. And you're the prettiest girl. You're looking marvellous!" he murmured in her ear.

She did not answer. Once she would have smiled up at him with starry eyes, but now her lashes remained obstinately lowered, silken fans upon her cheeks. Now that she was indifferent, she intrigued him far more than in the days when she had responded, swift and ardent, to his approaches, though in those days she had had the added attraction of being an heiress, whereas now . . . And yet those furs of hers were worth a pretty penny. Euan sensed a mystery. Had she been getting herself engaged—or married?—to some wealthy fellow? He would have a look at her left hand at the first opportunity. Meanwhile it was out of sight, behind his arm.

"What are you doing with yourself these days?" he asked.

"Earning my living." As a guest in someone's house she must be reasonably polite, but all the same she wouldn't say one word more than was necessary to be civil.

He raised his eyebrows. "Earning it remarkably successfully, by all appearances!"

No reply.

"D'you like your job?"

"Very much indeed."

"What d'you do?"

"I work in Harley Street."

"What as? Receptionist?"

"I'm employed by Barclay Davenport, the surgeon," she replied, then wished she hadn't told him; it was no concern of his.

Euan was silent for a moment as he steered her expertly among the dancers, trying to remember. Davenport . . . That was the fellow who had done a tricky operation recently on some wealthy fellow who had come to him at death's door from America. All the papers had been full of it.

"Davenport? One of the king-pins at his job! Young, too, isn't he?"

"Somewhere in the thirties." To speak of Barclay gave her a strange sensation, pleasure mixed with pain.

"Married?"

"No."

Had she changed color, very faintly? Was he on to something interesting? "I suppose it was from Barclay Davenport that you got those furs of yours?"

Now at last she did look up at him. He wouldn't have believed those shining eyes of hers could look so coldly scornful. "My dear Euan, I couldn't care less what you suppose! What an inquisitive old nosy parker you've grown into — or were you always, and I didn't notice?"

It was his turn now to flush — furious with her, yet attracted as he'd never been before. But as he was about to flare up in angry retort, the music stopped. Verity drew away from him and without another word or glance made her way swiftly through the dancers towards the door.

Lady Dunne was standing just inside the room, talking to two new arrivals. Here was the opportunity to do some introducing. She seized it.

"Miss Cator, this is Mr. Clive. And Major Lumley."

Ronald Clive, brown-haired and tall and thin, had a deep, drawling voice and twinkling eyes. Hugh Lumley was thickset, with a small fair clipped moustache and a pleasant expression. By the time Euan had caught up with Verity she was between the two of them, her back towards him, while they argued laughingly as to who should first dance with her.

"I met you first——"

"By a split second. And she looked at me first. Didn't you?" Major Lumley appealed to Verity.

"Let's do it by alphabetical order. C before L!" said Ronald Clive.

"And Hugh before Ronald!" said Hugh Lumley.

The music had begun again. Ronald Clive settled the problem by seizing Verity and dancing off with her, while Major Lumley called after her, "The next for me, please!"

Sulkily Euan found himself another partner, the daughter of the wealthy chairman of a firm of brewers. Coralie was an only child, shallow and spoilt. But as far as Euan was concerned her money outweighed these disadvantages, and since he had first met her a few weeks ago he had been pursuing her with matrimony in his mind. With reductions in the armed forces looming large, a wealthy wife, plus the probability of a nice job in a brewery, had considerable attractions.

Somehow these attractions seemed this evening to have lost much of their potency, and as he danced with Coralie he carefully manoeuvred her so as to keep Verity in view, irritably noting that she was obviously getting on well with Ronald Clive.

"I don't believe you're listening to a word I'm saying!" Coralie told him petulantly, after he had made several inappropriate replies to what she had been telling him about her poodle puppy and the new car her father had given her.

Euan laughed off the accusation. But it was true enough. He had been speculating about Verity, who looked so elegant and so prosperous; wondering whether the lawyers had managed to arrange things so that after all she had inherited at least a portion of her aunt's money . . . whether after all, she would have been a good catch, and he had been a fool to show his hand so soon, and lose a damned attractive girl who might not, after all, be penniless.

Was it too late to get her back? Admittedly she had been just about as snubbing as she could, without being actually uncivil. Still, she had been very smitten with him not too long ago. Could be that she still was; that her chilly manner had been an act assumed to hide her feelings, save her pride? He'd dance with her, try to get back into her good graces, and if possible find out how the land lay in regard to her finances.

To get a dance with Verity proved more difficult than he had expected. Even to get near her wasn't easy. Lady Dunne, an admirable hostess, took good care to bring up and introduce one man after another to her between dances, and she seemed to be continually either dancing or surrounded by would-be partners. Nor were matters made easier by the fact that she refused to catch his eye, no matter how he might try to attract her attention. Always as he reached her she would turn away, and talk to someone else. Always her gaze was fixed infuriatingly to right or left of him. The party neared its end, already a few people had left, and cups of hot soup had appeared upon the scene, before she turned, not knowing he was just behind her, and he seized the opportunity he had been waiting for.

"You've been avoiding me all evening!" he reproached her. "How about having the next dance wtih me?"

"I doubt if there will be another dance—and anyway, I'm leaving in a few minutes."

"I'll take you home, then."

Verity made no reply. She hoped to slip away without his seeing her, but as she turned away after saying good night to Lady Dunne, Euan was at her elbow, and without making a to-do it was impossible to prevent him leaving with her.

A sallow dark girl with a peevish expression called after him peremptorily, "Euan — if you'll wait a second while I get my coat, I'll give you a lift in the Rolls."

Almost imperceptibly he hesitated, then called back, "Sorry, Coralie — no can do! Thanks for suggesting it," and followed Verity.

Coralie stared after him with tightened lips, and nostrils flared with temper. Then she swung round to a dark, dapper young man called Peter Enderby, who had been her constant escort until Euan superseded him. "Want a lift, Peter?"

Peter lived in St. John's Wood, Coralie in Chelsea, and Lowndes Square lay midway between the two, but he accepted, outwardly nonchalant, inwardly delighted. My turn again, he thought. That fellow has cooked his goose with Coralie, and no mistake!

The early evening had been slightly foggy, though not enough to interfere with visibility. When Verity and Euan emerged on to the pavement they found that it had thickened, hiding the tall trees in the garden of the square. A taxi loomed towards them through its acrid yellowish gloom, hugging the curb. Euan hailed it, then opened the door for Verity to get in. No use arguing, she thought; there won't be many taxis out in this! She got in.

"Where to?" Euan asked her.

She told him, adding, "But there's not the slightest need for you to see me home!"

He ignored that, but passed on the address to the driver, adding, "And drive slowly!"

The man growled that it wasn't very likely anyone would go speeding on a night like this, as Euan got in and slammed the door.

"So you live with Davenport!" he said.

"Under the same roof, yes. So do his small niece and a middle-aged cousin."

"You disappoint me. I had hoped for something more romantic!"

"I should have said sordid was a better word for what you are implying!" she retorted. As he slid an arm along the seat behind her, she added, "If you try to paw me I shall scream, and tell the driver that you're making a nuisance of yourself!"

Sulkily Euan withdrew his arm. "I'd never have believed a girl could change so much in such a short time! You used to be so—so——"

"So gullible that I didn't see through you! And now I'm not. And I do. And you don't like it. Too bad! *Poor Euan!*" she teased him.

Euan was the type to whom elusiveness is magnetic, and the unattainable far more desirable than the accessible. In her mood of mockery Verity attracted him infinitely more than in the days when she had been responsive.

Supposing that she *had* inherited some of her aunt's money, after all—? It couldn't be a fraction of what Coralie would have and Verity had no plum job at her disposal. None the less . . .

Turning on all the charm at his command, he said, "Look, Verity, you might be fair to a chap! You must admit it wasn't I who broke off our engagement. *You* did, in a huff, when I was trying to explain that as your aunt had left you nothing after all, we'd have to wait a bit before we could afford to marry. I would have been a thorough-going cad to let you in for life upon a captain's pay and precious little else, now wouldn't I? But you wouldn't let me finish. Up you got on your high horse and broke it off . . ."

"Does it matter how it happened? It *did* get broken off, which is all that counts!" Verity yawned. "Oh, dear— what *is* the matter with this taxi? It's simply *crawling!*"

Now they were turning into Harley Street. Another minute and I shall be safely back in my own world, under the same roof as Barclay! Verity was thinking.

Euan thought: another minute and she will be gone, and I'll have lost my chance to fix up a reconciliation with her — queered my pitch with Coralie for nothing. He said, with a sincerity that surprised himself, "Now that I've found you after all this time, let's keep in touch. Will you come out with me one evening very soon, to show there's no hard feeling? Dinner and dance — a play and supper after? Anything you like."

Verity was going to refuse. Then the thought flashed through her mind — What would be the effect on Barclay, if he were to see me as a girl who doesn't spend her evenings knitting in the nursery — a girl who's in demand, a girl invited out by such a personable spark as Euan?

Almost she accepted Euan's invitation. But suddenly she knew she couldn't do it. If Barclay didn't come to love her in the natural course of things, she wasn't going to try to draw his interest by a cheap and artificial ruse.

She said, "It's kind of you to suggest it, Euan. But I'm afraid, to use your own expression, 'No can do'."

Sulkily he demanded, "Why not?"

She shrugged her shoulders. "I've outgrown you, with a lot of other things abandoned in my callow past!"

"But dammit, Verity——"

The taxi stopped, preventing any further argument. She had her latchkey ready. Sometimes it stuck, and one had to manoeuvre with it, getting it in just far enough but not too far. Tonight it turned without an effort. She was thankful. Clumsy fumblings would have spoilt her exit.

" 'night, Euan! It's been amusing, seeing you again!" said Verity, and shut the door upon his sulky face, reflecting with considerable satisfaction that in this last encounter with him she had had the best of it.

This evening had avenged the past more than she would ever know. Next morning Euan tried to telephone to Coralie, only to be told by an impressive butler that she was engaged and could not speak to him. The same thing happened later that day, and again that evening, and on the following day as well. He wrote, inviting her to dine and dance at the Savoy, but had a curt refusal. And a week later her engagement to Peter Enderby was announced.

Euan found the experience of falling heavily between two stools as unpleasant as his worst enemy — and he had quite a number of them — could have wished.

Coughing a little, for even in the short way from the taxi to the door she had breathed in the acrid fumes of fog, Verity went up in the lift. She didn't feel inclined to walk up two long flights of stairs, after all that dancing!

Usually the top floor was comfortably warm. Tonight it

seemed so chilly that she wondered whether something could have gone wrong with the radiator that warmed it, but when she felt it with her hand its temperature seemed much the same as usual.

Funny, she thought — the passage reeks of fog! It must be thicker than I realized, and colder, too. I've never known it to get right inside like this, so damp and raw and penetrating!

Then, as she reached the room she shared with Julia, she understood. Always she left the door ajar throughout the evening, so that she might hear Julia if she called for her. Because of this, she kept the windows shut until she went to bed, otherwise an icy draught swept through, chilling the rooms and all the rest of the top floor as well. When she went out she had as usual left the door a few inches ajar, Miss Duncan having said that she would listen for Julia if she should call. Now it was opened to its full extent. Two heavy books had been so placed on the floor as to hold it. The windows, which she had left tightly shut, were opened wide. The fog was pouring in, clammy and dank and acrid, making her eyes smart, stinging her nostrils, harsh and irritating in her lungs.

As Verity rushed across the room to close the windows, she remembered how time and again Miss Duncan had disparaged Julia's "pasty face," said that they must turn her into "a nice rosy little English girl," hinted that she did not have enough fresh air, asked if they always had their bedroom windows opened at night. Obviously it was she who had done this, and one must try to look on it as well-meaning zeal on her part, though exasperating interference did seem a more appropriate term! Probably the fog had come down in its present density after she had gone to bed. Still, fog or no fog, to leave both door and windows wide upon a winter's evening in a room where a small child lay asleep was scarcely wise.

Anxiously Verity bent over Julia. She was sound asleep. One hand and arm, clasping a teddy bear, lay uncovered. Gently Verity drew the bedclothes over her, tucking them round her neck, dismayed to feel the icy coldness of the little hand. She turned on the electric fire, hoping the room would soon warm up, although the foggy fumes might linger.

Shivering, she decided that the quickest way to warm herself would be in a hot bath, and lying in the steaming water mused upon the curious turns and twists of life. Had this happened a few short months ago, as she lay here she would have been re-living all the pleasures of the party — gay encounters, haunting music, youth and laughter. Yet now, because of Barclay's absence from the party it had meant no more to her than taking Julia to buy a pair of shoes, and less than Julia's enjoyment of an outing to the Zoo.

Darling, funny little Julia! Verity smiled to herself, picturing her grave dark eyes, her silky hair, the sudden flashing smile she shared with Barclay; feeling in imagination the stranglehold of her thin little arms hugging her good night with a surprising strength for one so fragile. Then she frowned, thinking of the last word that had passed through her mind. Fragile. That fragility of hers was worrying. Though she had put on over two pounds since she arrived in England, still she looked as though she had been made of thistledown and moonbeams. Anything so small and frail could surely put up little in the way of resistance against illness, if it came her way. With all her heart Verity hoped the little girl had taken no harm from the bitter, acrid air in which she must have lain for nearly three hours: Miss Duncan usually went to bed at ten, and it had been close on one when Verity returned and shut the windows.

She told herself it was ridiculous to cross one's bridges before reaching them, that a thin child was often wiry, that if Julia did catch cold it wasn't anything to fuss about, but quite a normal happening in any nursery, and anyway they had a doctor on the spot, and by the time she went back to the bedroom her anxiety had subsided. Although the air still smelt unpleasantly of fog, the room was warmer now, and she felt reassured to see that Julia still slept peacefully.

Verity got into bed and put the light out. She was drowsing into sleep when suddenly she was jolted wide awake by the sound of a small dry cough.

She told herself it was ridiculous to worry. Julia might have a tickle. Perhaps her throat was dry from sleeping with her mouth open. None the less, she lay for a time tensely listening. And presently she heard a second little cough, followed this time by a small voice saying questioningly, "Verity?"

In a moment she had turned the light on and was by the other bed. "Here I am, darling. Are you thirsty?"

Julia sighed, then gave another little rasping cough. "My froat feels funny," she complained. "Can I have a drink?"

"Of course you can! I tell you what — I'll give you hot milk with some honey in it, that's splendid for a tickly throat. You cuddle down and keep warm. I won't be long."

"I'm warm already. I'm *too* warm!" Julia complained. Verity smoothed back the silky wisps of dark hair from her forehead. It felt burning hot beneath her touch. Her heart sank. "All the same, keep covered up, or when I come back you'll be turned into an icicle and all that nice milk will be wasted — it's a horrid cold night!"

"It *would* be a surprise for you to find an icicle astead of me!" said Julia, and coughed again.

The kitchen clock ticked in a cosy, comfortable voice that had a reassuring sound. The breakfast tray was laid all ready for tomorrow morning — no, this morning! There were fish cakes on a plate, ready to be fried. It all looked very normal, very safe and homely. Yet Verity's hands were none too steady as she poured milk in a saucepan and spooned honey from a jar. Don't let her be ill . . . Please, *please* don't let Julia be ill! she prayed, her face cupped in her hands while she was waiting for the milk to heat.

"Anything wrong?"

Barclay was standing in the doorway. His hands were thrust deep in the pockets of a tailored dressing gown of dark blue, with facings of a lighter blue.

Verity cried in tones of heartfelt thankfulness, "I'm sorry for disturbing you — but oh, I *am* so glad that you're awake!"

CHAPTER TWELVE

"I saw the light was still on in the passage, and wondered if you had got back all right," Barclay explained. In dressing gown and blue pyjamas, with his dark hair for once a little rumpled, he looked even taller than usual. "What are you up to?" he demanded.

"I'm getting a hot drink for Julia. — Oh, I do *wish* I hadn't gone!" Verity exclaimed miserably. "When I got back, I found the bedroom windows as wide open as they'd go. They must have been like that for hours. The room was thick with fog, and icy cold—the door was open too, and so there was a frightful draught. And Julia has begun to cough. She says her throat 'feels funny.' And her forehead's burning hot — I'm sure she has a temperature. Oh, I *shouldn't* have gone out and left her!"

"Blaming yourself for something that's no fault of yours won't make things any better. What's that you're brewing up for her?"

"Honey and hot milk."

"I'll go and take her temperature before she has it."

Alone again, Verity flushed crimson with vexation as she stirred the honey in the milk. Idiot that I am! she thought — I ought to have remembered that her temperature is bound to go up after a hot drink. Oh, what a ninny he must think me, not to have taken it first!

A voice behind her said, "Your own throat will be 'feeling funny' next, if you don't keep warm! Better put this on." Barclay was holding out a tweed coat he must have taken from her wardrobe. She slid her arms into the sleeves; the thin sleeves of her dressing gown went in without much trouble. Barclay helped her into it. Had his hands really lingered on her shoulders in the briefest of caresses, or was her imagination working overtime in her wrought-up state of mind?

He went away again. Verity followed him a moment later with the hot drink. She found him sitting on the end of Julia's bed quietly talking to her, while the little girl, thermometer in mouth, gazed at him with heavy eyes. Her cheeks were flushed. Anxiously, but with little hope, Verity waited for the verdict when at last Barclay took the thermometer and examined it, then shook it down. He did not look at Verity.

"Have I got a tempitture?" Asked Julia in a hoarse little voice.

"Just a bit," he told her.

The corners of her mouth turned down. "Will I have to stay in bed tomorrow?"

"'Fraid so! People who have temperatures can't go running round, you know, or they get ill."

Tears brimmed in the heavy eyes, but before they could spill over Verity said quickly, "We'll pretend that you're in hospital! What fun! I'll be the nurse — I'll wear a white veil on my head, the way they do——"

"And I'll pretend to be the doctor," Barclay followed up, "and listen to your chest, and tell the nurse what medicines to give you."

The tears were blinked away, though Julia's mouth was tremulous still. "Can the medicine be pretend, too— not real? I don't like medicine. It has a nashty taste!"

"You can have a pill to start with. That won't taste at all. I'll get it right away. And Verity has brought you a delicious drink with honey in it."

Presently, when the pill had been washed down with milk and honey, and Julia, clasping the cup in both hands, had drunk what remained of her hot drink, Barclay told her, "Now we're going to tuck you up, and you must go to sleep again while I give Verity a hot drink. It's her turn, don't you think?"

"And you too?" Julia asked, as Verity turned her pillow and drew the bedclothes cosily about her neck.

"I expect so! Good night—sleep tight . . ."

"Pleasant dreams — all night!" Julia finished for him. As they looked back at her from the door she was already dropping off into an uneasy doze.

"What's her temperature?" Verity demanded when they were out of earshot in the passage.

"Might be a lot worse. Just over a hundred. Nothing really for a child. They rocket up for nothing, and drop down again in no time. She may be down to normal in the morning. Probably you've nipped the trouble in the bud."

"It need never have begun, if only I hadn't gone to that stupid party; I shall never forgive myself if Julia is really ill—it'll be all my fault!" she told him wretchedly.

"Don't be a little goose! The fault is Margaret's, if it's anyone's. But when trouble comes it doesn't help to argue about who's to blame." He opened the refrigerator. "Plenty of milk here, anyway. What are you going to have? The same as Julia?"

"I don't want——" she began, but Barclay cut her short.

"No good saying you don't want anything. This is doctor's orders. Honey and hot milk it is!" He measured out a cup of milk into a saucepan. "Where did you put that honey?"

"Don't you bother — I can do it for myself!" Verity protested. But he took no notice, found the honey, and stirred some in the milk as deftly as though the kitchen were as much his province as the operating theatre.

"Drink that after you're in bed," he told her, "and be sure you call me if you're worried about Julia. She's pretty sure to sleep the night through — that pill I gave her was a mild sedative. Good night!"

Tired though she was, Verity could not sleep. She lay awake a long time, listening to Julia tossing restlessly, waiting tensely for that little rasping cough, rising every now and then to make sure she was covered up, and dreading what tomorrow might bring forth. In spite of Barclay's reassurance, she could sense he was as anxious as she was herself.

She fell asleep at last, to be awakened shortly before seven by a little hoarse voice saying plaintively, "Verity! Are you awake? I'm firsty! Can I have a drink?"

Scarcely knowing how she had got there, Verity found herself beside the other bed. "Of course, darling! What would you like? Some nice cold orange juice?"

She laid her hand on Julia's forehead. It was burning hot; the heavy eyes were bright with fever and the small face, usually pale, was flushed. Her heart sank.

Julia said she would like orange juice. As Verity went to get it in the kitchen, Barclay appeared, looking as though he had been up and dressed for hours.

"How are things?" he asked.

"Not too good, I'm afraid."

"I'll go and have a look at her."

As she squeezed oranges Verity sent up a heartfelt prayer of thanksgiving that he was there, a tower of strength, expert and kind, to take responsibility for the sick child.

When she went back to the bedroom he had taken Julia's temperature. Answering the question in her eyes, he murmured, "Up to 103. I'll sound her chest." Aloud, he said, "Now then, Nurse, what about getting dressed and putting on your uniform? Tell me when you're ready and I'll bring my stethoscope and overhaul the patient."

"Could you lend me an enormous handkerchief, a white one, for my head?"

"I'll find you an outsize one." Barclay turned to Julia. "You may have your orange juice, Miss Staverley," he told her gravely, "and when Nurse is ready I will come and have a look at you."

"Like doctors do in hospital?"

"Just like doctors do in hospital," he assured her.

Julia lay back on her pillows as he went to get the handkerchief. "Unkoo Barclay called me 'Miss Staverley'!"

"You'd better call him 'Mr. Davenport' as long as you're in hospital."

"And you'll be Nurse!"

Julia's sigh of satisfaction turned into a little hard cough. Her small face crumpled. "It hurt me!" she complained. Verity's heart was heavy as she dressed.

When some fifteen minutes later she went to summon Barclay, she was looking very professional in her white overall, with his handkerchief as coif.

"I don't want any breakfuss," Julia murmured as he sounded her small skinny chest.

"I'll tell Nurse you can go without for once," he reassured her. "Come with me a minute, will you, Nurse? I want to give you some instructions."

A little crooked smile curved Julia's mouth. She thought she would have been enjoying the game, if only she didn't feel so funny. As the door closed behind Verity and Barclay, she drifted off again into a restless doze.

The drawing-room at this hour of the morning looked as forlorn as Verity was feeling. Miss Duncan had not troubled to plump up cushions and straighten chairs before she went to bed last night, as Verity had always done for Mrs. Davenport, and the remains of last night's fire looked cheerless.

Their eyes met, Verity's filled with desperate enquiry, Barclay's grave. Verity breathed, "Is she—very bad?"

"She's not too good. Looks like pneumonia, I'm afraid. I'm going to get Reith-Galloway, the children's specialist, to come along as soon as possible. Meanwhile we can only keep her warm and comfortable. Give her drinks, a little at a time, if she should want them. Nothing in the way of treatment until Reith-Galloway has seen her. I'll ring him up at once."

Mrs. Bream and Ellen were arriving as Verity left the drawing-room. They looked wide-eyed, as well they might, at Verity in her nurse's garb. She told them, "Julia's ill— we're playing at hospital, that's why I'm all dressed up!"

As the two kindly women were exclaiming in concern, Miss Duncan came forth from her bedroom, going to her bath. "Whatever is going on here?" she demanded, looking disapproving. Her hair was covered with a yellow plastic cap, her broad face glistened with an application of skin food (who would have thought, to look at her, that she took trouble with her appearance?) and a grey dressing gown was tied by a wide sash where her waist, if she had had one, would have been.

Verity explained a second time that Julia was ill, and they were playing that she was in hospital, "so I'm dressed up as nurse."

Miss Duncan blinked her sandy lashes disapprovingly. "Ill? Surely this is very sudden! There was nothing wrong

141

with her last night—when I looked in last night before I went to bed I found her sound asleep."

Verity was silent. If I speak, she thought, I'll say too much.

Miss Duncan went on, "This is what comes of coddling her! This may be a lesson to you. Perhaps in future you will take advice from those with more experience than yourself!"

Barclay had finished telephoning. He arrived to hear her last words, while Mrs. Bream and Ellen tactfully disappeared into the kitchen and shut the door behind them.

"My dear Margaret, the less advice we have from you the better! Julia's illness is entirely your fault."

"*My* fault, indeed . . .!" Miss Duncan gasped, scarlet with astonishment and indignation.

"Yes—yours! Last night, although there was a thick fog, in spite of all you must have read and heard of illness —yes, and death—due to fog, you opened her bedroom windows wide as they would go, though Verity had very wisely left them closed. You even left the door wide, too, so as to ensure a draught! You couldn't well have done the thing more thoroughly if it had been your deliberate intent to make Julia ill. She must have lain for hours in the raw air, thick with smog—the whole flat reeked of it by the time I came upon the scene, although by then Verity had shut the windows. I dislike recriminations, but you have brought this on yourself by blaming Verity for what was caused entirely by your interference."

Miss Duncan changed her ground. "So you would blame *me* for Julia's illness! All because the girl you pay to care for her went gadding to a party, leaving me to do her work!"

She shrank back from the look in Barclay's eyes, clutching her sponge and towel, a ludicrous figure in the plastic cap that nearly matched her freckles, as he said, "No more of that! You've said too much already. There's trouble enough, without your making more."

"Trouble! I'm sure I never meant——"

"You came here on the understanding that you would make other plans as soon as possible. Have you anything in view?"

"Not yet — I thought ——" her voice trailed into incoherency.

"You thought if you did nothing about it you might remain here permanently, I suppose! No. I'm sorry, Margaret, but there is a limit to my patience, and you've strained it too far. I'd like you to arrange to leave as soon as you can find somewhere else to go."

Dr. Gairloch, returning to her flat shortly before lunch, was not best pleased when her housekeeper told her that Miss Duncan had been waiting for some time to see her. Her visitor, however, was too wrought up to realize that Janice was annoyed to find her here, her dowdy, dumpy figure as incongruous in the elegant room as a sparrow in a flock of humming birds.

Breathlessly she poured out her story in disjointed sentences. Julia had pneumonia—Barclay had called in a children's specialist—they were getting a night nurse. "The whole thing is entirely That Girl's fault! She went out to a party last night, if you please, and asked me if I would see to Julia if she cried . . . "

"Why should her absence cause Julia to contract pneumonia?"

Reluctantly Margaret Duncan told her of the opened windows. "Everybody knows that children need fresh air! If That Girl hadn't coddled her and made her soft, it would have done no harm. I simply did my duty — and now I'm blamed for it, and Barclay wants me to go somewhere else as soon as I can manage to arrange it."

She had been hoping Janice would at once invite her to move down one floor and stay with her indefinitely. Janice, however, did no such thing. Secretly she was not ill pleased that Margaret might be leaving. She had been no help in getting rid of Verity, and her continual dropping in was tiresome. Looking distastefully at Margaret's podgy face, which never failed to make her think of suet crust, she said, "In that case, the sooner you get on with it, the better! Barclay's not the sort to change his mind! —Sorry to turn you out, my dear, but I must lunch now. My next appointment is at two."

Then, as she was going towards the door, a sudden thought occurred to her. Her manner became more friendly as she said, "A child as delicate as Julia appears to be would be far better out of London, once she has recovered."

The two women looked at one another. Margaret Duncan said, "But Barclay mightn't think of that . . ."

"Possibly not. But someone might suggest it to him. And if Julia were ordered convalescence by the sea, or in the country, 'That Girl' would have to go too. And in that case, Barclay might be glad of you to run the household for him, as you did before . . . I'd bide my time, if I were you, before you make new plans. Let matters drift and see what happens."

Miss Duncan brightened, then looked dubious. "You said yourself that Barclay's not the sort to change his mind. Supposing he insists that I must go?"

"Wait until he does insist, before you cross that bridge! I daresay for the present he will be too taken up with Julia to do anything about it."

"Maybe. But when she's getting better——"

"When she's getting better we must see what can be done to get her—and of course the Cator girl—away from London."

As she closed the door behind her now considerably less lugubrious visitor, Janice Gairloch was frowning. Now that she had no longer any hope of marrying Barclay Davenport, she would be glad to see the last of Margaret Duncan. As a permanency overhead she would be a nuisance rather than an asset, always dropping in when one least wanted her, for ever pressing her unfounded claims of friendship — stupid, tiresome woman that she was! Without compunction one must drop her. But before then she might serve one last purpose, be of use in helping to get rid of Verity Cator. Dr. Gairloch entirely understood the feelings of the fabled dog in the manger. Since Barclay Davenport was not for her, neither should that little interloper have him.

Julia was very ill indeed. During the next week Dr. Reith-Galloway came twice most days, and once three times. For Verity the days and nights merged into one another in a long exhausting nightmare. From the first Barclay had decreed she could not be in charge of Julia by day and night as well. He had engaged a nurse to take responsibility at night, and Ellen volunteered to sit with her by day when Verity was having a meal. But always it was Verity she called for, only Verity who could persuade her she must take her "nashty medicine," coax her to have a spoonful of chicken jelly, soothe her when she was fretful.

Worst of her memories of that anxious time would always be the dreadful day when in response to the small hoarse voice calling her name she bent above the sick child saying gently, "Here I am, darling!" — the brilliant eyes that looked so much too large for the small pinched face stared at her unrecognizingly and Julia whispered, "Go away—I don't want you! It's Verity I want!" — And there was nothing for it but to go away, and leave the nurse to try to soothe her.

Out in the passage she gave way at last. The tears that had for days lain heavy behind her aching eyes brimmed over. Leaning against the wall, face cupped in hands, she wept, too stupefied by weariness and grief to hear the quick elastic stride that took the stairs two steps at a time, as Barclay, between two appointments, came to see how Julia was faring. She had no idea that he was near her until his voice beside her said, sharpened a little by anxiety, "What's wrong? Is she worse?"

Between her sobs she said, "She—doesn't know me!"

Barclay took her in his arms and held her as one holds a grieving child, murmuring comfort, telling her that a child who one day seemed at death's door often was miraculously better twenty-four hours later, that "a skinny little scrap" like Julia often had better powers of recovery and was more wiry than a sturdier child. Sighing, she relaxed at last against his shoulder, too spent to be aware of anything save the peace and comfort of his presence.

How long had passed she did not know when presently he put her gently from him. "Better?"

"Much . . . Sorry I was such a—such a donkey!"

"Where's Margaret?"

"Out, I think."

"Is she being a nuisance to you still? If so, I'll tell her she must leave at once, whether she has made other arrangements or not."

"No—oh, no! I scarcely see her, and she's taken on the housekeeping. To turn her out would do no good to Julia, and that's all that matters now. And you'd feel bad about it after—you would remember how your mother felt about her . . ."

"All right. No need to get worked up about it!" Barclay soothed her. "Now go and rest. I can stay here for an hour or so, and anyway Nurse Reid is very good with her, and Reith-Galloway will be coming again early in the afternoon. Try not to worry —probably today will be the turning point and after this she'll begin making headway."

He was right. The worst was over. Julia slept all that afternoon, and when she waked gave Verity a drowsy smile of recognition, and actually ate some chicken jelly without any coaxing. Three days later Nurse Reid departed to another case, Dr. Reith-Galloway cut down his visits, Julia announced that she was "tired of playing hospital," and transformed herself from being a patient in a ward into a fisherman in a boat. The bedroom floor became the sea, Verity was continually warned "step on the islands" —(mats)— "or you'll be drowned!" At least once a day Barclay, visiting the little patient, brought her some amusing trifle which, while Verity distracted her attention, he fixed upon the curtain hook upon her "line" — a piece of string supplied by Mrs. Bream — to be caught later by the excited fisherman.

So the time came when once again Miss Duncan dropped in upon her friend on the first floor, to say that Julia had been up this morning, and that the time was ripe to talk of sending her away from London. "Barclay has said no more about my leaving. I've kept house while Julia has been ill, so if we can get rid of That Girl, with any luck I shall stay on for good. Should I suggest to Barclay that a child is better in the country? Tell him about that little school I heard about at Frimley?"

"Better keep out of it. You'll only make a mess of it." said Dr. Gairloch bluntly. "Leave it to me. I'll drop in this evening and see how the land lies. Barclay will be in around six, I take it?"

"He's sure to be with Julia then. He always is. She's settled for the night at half-past."

"Right! I'll see what I can do."

"I'll back you up in anything you say."

"Far better hold your tongue and leave it all to me."

Miss Duncan went away, resentfully reflecting that Janice sometimes spoke to her as if she were a child — and a half-witted child, at that!

Julia was allowed up again that afternoon, though she was back in bed again by five. Barclay was playing snakes and ladders with her, while Verity looked on, when following a tap upon the door Miss Duncan appeared. "Here's a visitor for Julia—and she's brought a most exciting present!" she announced, and made way for Dr. Gairloch, who entered carrying a glass bowl with four goldfish, which she had sent her housekeeper to buy. Julia was enchanted, and it would have been churlish not to make the visitor welcome. Verity put her own chair into a convenient place for her, and withdrew into the background.

Never had she seen Dr. Gairloch appear to better advantage than during the next quarter of an hour. She laid herself out to be agreeable to Julia, talking to the child as though they were alone together, discussing with her what to call the goldfish. It was only when she rose to go that at long last she turned to Barclay. "Where are you going to send her for her convalescence?"

"Where do you suggest?" he countered, pleasantly enough.

"Sidmouth has a very pleasant winter climate. Or Torquay — or Bognor——"

"Winter? But we're practically into spring! It's nearly April," he reminded her.

"My dear man, when have you ever seen a sign of spring in Harley Street? . . . If she were *my* child, I'd keep her permanently in the country.—Good night, Julia!"

She did not glance at Verity as she turned towards the door.

Barclay followed her. He did not close the door behind them: Verity could hear them talking in the passage. Janice Gairloch declared, "I mean it, Barclay! Julia isn't fit to stand up to our fogs and petrol fumes and all the rest of it. A child as frail as that should have a country life. The sooner she leaves here, the better for her!"

Her heart lurched sickeningly and missed a beat, then began racing wildly, as with a pang of shock she heard him answer, "Thanks for the good advice, Janice. You will be glad to hear that I intend to take it. I shall arrange for Julia to leave here for the country or the sea as soon as she is fit to travel."

CHAPTER THIRTEEN

WITH Julia, looking even more fragile than before her illness, and a good half-inch taller, skipping happily beside her, Verity walked up Harley Street upon an April morning.

She was wondering how long it would be before she came this way again. Never, perhaps! For her two enemies Janice Gairloch and her catspaw Margaret Duncan, had won their subtle war against her. Julia had recovered, and Barclay, following the advice Dr. Gairloch had given him unasked, had arranged for Verity to take her to recuperate in a small hotel on the east coast, where they were to stay for an unspecified time. She had begun to doubt whether he intended them to return to London. The presence of a small child in his home must be disrupting to his bachelor existence, and probably the silent conflict between Verity and his cousin was a constant irritant.

Would he, when they had been absent for a week or two and Julia was fully recovered, tell her he had made other plans for his small niece? That he was sending her to share a country home with other children? Or to some little school with children of her own age? Or——?

"Verity—you're not *listening* to me!" Julia complained. She had been chattering away ever since they had set forth to do some final shopping.

Verity apologized. "I'm sorry, darling! I was thinking. What were you saying?"

"I were asking if it will be springtime when we get to Southwold? Mrs. Bream says spring's the nicest time of all the year."

"It's spring already!" Verity told her.

Julia looked about her in surprise. "Is it? How can anybody see it is? It looks the same as any other time?"

And she was right. No sign of spring was to be seen.

The houses rose on either side like steep grey cliffs. A chilly wind blew round the corners. The sky, though clear of clouds, was veiled by London's pall of smoke. There were no flowers in sight, no singing birds. Spring had not come to Harley Street!

Probably, thought Verity, it never does and never will. And for me, too, it's the same—spring has passed me by, beyond recall. Although at journey's end the sea may sparkle, larks soar singing up towards blue skies, daisies scatter the emerald grass like white confetti, in my heart it will be winter still . . .

As they approached the door it opened, and Dr. Gairloch came out, immaculate as ever in a new spring suit of willow green that emphasized the curious greenish pallor of her face, her pale gold hair so sleek and smooth as to resemble metal, ear-rings in the shape of small gold bows in the long lobes of her ears. Her pale cold eyes were glittering with triumph undisguised as they met Verity's.

Her metallic voice bade them good morning. She went on, "I hear you will be leaving soon. When are you off?"

Both she and Verity knew that what she really meant was, "I have won, you see! I'm getting rid of you at last! I shall be here, in the same house as Barclay, when you are far away. I belong to his world, share his interests. Who knows . . . ?"

Verity, determined to betray no sign of what she suffered, held her head high and met the older woman's probing eyes composedly as she replied that they were going tomorrow morning. "So we should be there in time for lunch."

"By road or rail?"

She answered that the chauffeur would be taking them by road, and said that she and Julia were looking forward very much to being by the sea.

Janice Gairloch made a little grimace of distaste. "Rather you than I! To me, the sea is boring beyond words. Except, of course, at Cap d'Antibes, or Juan les Pins, or somewhere of that sort."

"How lucky," Verity replied, "that it takes all sorts to make a world! One must miss so much fun by being blasée! I suppose that's what the saying means—'Whom the Gods love, die young.' Young in heart."

Janice Gairloch looked as a poisonous snake might if a kitten turned upon it with unleashed claws. It did Verity good to see the fury in her eyes, although the tiny triumph could not alter—nothing could, now!—the fact that on the main issue between them she was vanquished and the older woman victor.

She said to Julia, "Say good-bye to Dr. Gairloch, darling. We must go now, Mrs. Bream is waiting for the fish for lunch."

Julia held out a small frail hand politely. "Good-bye!"

Dr. Gairloch touched it perfunctorily. "Good-bye, Julia. Good-bye, Miss Cator. I don't suppose that we shall meet again." The smile that stretched her thin-lipped mouth but did not light her eyes was venomous as she added mockingly, "Too, *too* sad!" and turned away to hail a taxi.

Julia said, as they crossed the hall, "I don't *like* that lady!"

Verity would have loved her even more for it, had that been possible. "Don't you, darling? Why not?"

Julia considered it before explaining, "Maybe it's acause *she* doesn't like *me* . . . I don't b'leeve she likes *any*body!"

Would the door of the consulting room be opened as they passed? It was three days since Verity had seen Barclay, though his voice had reached her sometimes in the nursery, speaking to Julia or Ellen, or on the telephone. But the door remained shut.

Upstairs Miss Duncan was energetically sorting out the contents of the linen cupboard, with a sulky Ellen in attendance. She had told Verity two days ago, "My cousin wants me to keep house for him again, so I will take over right away."

Verity had answered, "As you please," thinking that Barclay might have told her himself what had been arranged. How could she have supposed that he had liked her even mildly? Tomorrow she was going away, perhaps forever; yet since Julia had been able to resume her normal life a week ago, seeing her uncle of an evening in the sitting-room, so that there was no occasion for him to visit the nursery, he had sought no opportunity of seeing Verity, and had scarcely exchanged more than two words with her. And when he had, they had concerned the details of tomorrow's journey.

Intelligence waged war in her with instinct, trying to persuade her that to leave here was the best thing that could happen to her. She was young, with life ahead; gradually her thoughts of him would lose their poignancy as she picked up other threads, and in the end she would forget him as new interests grew up around her. So said her head. Her heart refused to be convinced, longing to remain here, under the same roof with him, living in the hope of seeing him, hearing his voice, discussing with him some domestic detail, gaining some small comfort from his presence, no matter how indifferent he might be to hers; able now and then when no one was about, to steal into his room and lay her cheek against his dressing gown that hung behind the door, lay light fingers in a brief caress on the ivory brushes he had used that morning.

Miss Duncan pounced upon her. "Oh, *there* you are! I thought you'd both been kidnapped, you and Julia, you've been such an age! Just as well I didn't wait to check the linen till you'd gone — there are all kinds of mysteries that Ellen can't or won't explain, but you may clear them up.

These double damask napkins with the rose design — how is it there are only nine left? There were ten when I was here before! — Ellen, you may go."

Handing Ellen the parcel of fish for Mrs. Bream, Verity explained, "The laundry lost the tenth."

"Oh. I see." Miss Duncan appeared almost disappointed to be given such a simple explanation, but returned to the attack. "And what about those two very pretty bedspreads that were in the room you sleep in now with Julia? Lilac taffeta, they were. I see the ones there now are rose-pink candlewick. Where are the others?"

"The taffeta had perished, and they split to ribbons. Mrs. Davenport had them put out soon after I came here. They weren't even fit to give a jumble sale."

Miss Duncan gave her a suspicious look, as though suspecting her of having packed away the missing bedspreads, good as new, among her luggage, opened her mouth to say something, but thought better of it, and began putting back with pudgy freckled hands the linen she had taken from its shelves, less neatly than it had been arranged before. "Oh, well—I shall get things reorganized in time," she said ungraciously, "and it is not as though we didn't know where you are going. If anything is missing, we can always write and ask you for an explanation. — You may go now!"

For a moment anger blazed in Verity. She kept it in control. It died as swiftly as it had risen. What did Miss Duncan's insults matter, after all? What did anything matter, save time was ticking past relentlessly, a stream of seconds adding into minutes, then to hours, towards the moment when she must say good-bye to Barclay, possibly forever? She turned away without a word.

Barclay came back earlier than usual that evening for his final playtime with his small niece, and because of this Julia, who always listened for the sound of his return, was taken by surprise, and did not hear him coming and rush out as usual to meet him, so he came to fetch her.

Julia, who had been absorbed in putting the last stitches in a pig depicted on a card, whose outline she had been for days embroidering in scarlet to give him as a parting present, hastily thrust it for concealment up her jersey, hoping Uncle Barry hadn't seen it. Luckily he seemed to notice nothing as he smiled at her. "I've come back early, so we'll have a bit of extra time together on your last night here," he told her. "Ready?"

"In a minute." Hands pressed to her jersey lest the precious card should slip from hiding, she slid down from her seat, went to a chair, and with back turned to him so that he should not see what she was doing, pushed the card beneath a cushion.

Julia need not have worried. Barclay was not watching her. He was looking at Verity, who was putting fresh shelf paper in an emptied cupboard, determined that Miss Duncan should have no excuse for saying she had left things in disorder — although like as not she'd say it anyway!

"All packed up?" he asked.

She would not look at him, for sudden tears had pricked her eyes. Keeping her voice under careful control, she said, "Yes! all except a few last-minute things."

Barclay said, "I'd like a word with you before you go. There won't be time for that tomorrow morning. Will it be all right with you, if I look in for a few minutes after dinner?"

"Of course." Now that she had blinked back the tears she met his eyes. They looked back into hers, darkly inscrutable as ever, searching, yet betraying nothing of his thoughts, no sign of whether he were glad that so soon he would be rid of her and Julia, or cared but little one way or the other. "Of course!" she repeated, "I shall be here all evening."

Waiting for him a couple of hours later, Verity felt restless. The packing finished, everything in order, there was nothing that needed to be done. She could not settle to a book, but wandered restlessly about the room, moving an ornament an inch or two and then replacing it exactly where it had stood before, altering the angle of a chair, twitching a curtain into place, until at last she heard the familiar sound of his approaching footsteps in their swift, impatient stride.

Barclay began by telling her of the arrangements he had made for her to draw what money she might need by cheques on an account he had opened for that purpose in a Southwold bank—which sounded, she reflected desolately, like a long-term arrangement.

"I heard this morning from those friends of mine, the Falconers, who live a few miles inland. They want you and Julia to——"

But Verity had no interest whatever in the Falconers, nor what kind of plans they had made for Julia and herself. Desperately she was trying to imprint every loved, familiar detail of him in her mind, to treasure there forever: shapely head so proudly poised upon his broad, flat shoulders, determined mouth that could be arrogant and yet could soften to tenderness when he spoke to Julia, or of her, grey eyes so deeply set as to seem darker than in fact they were. And above all those hands of his, muscular and flexible, combining delicacy with the strength of steel . . .

"*Verity!*" his voice broke through her thoughts. Barclay was looking at her with mingled puzzlement and concern. "You haven't taken in a single word of all I've said for the last five minutes! Feeling all right?" he asked.

"I—oh, yes! Perfectly all right! It's only that I—I——"

"Sit down. I can't imagine why you have been standing all this time while I've harangued you. Nor why I allowed you to!"

Muttering something about letting in a bit of air, he strode towards the window.

Yesterday Verity had noticed that a window cord had broken, and since matters of that sort were now no longer her affair, had told Miss Duncan, who had said that she would have it seen to. But nothing had been done. As Barclay pulled the upper sash down, the second cord broke, and the sash fell with a crash.

Almost simultaneously Verity, her first thought that it might have trapped his hands, started towards him, crying, "*Barry!* Darling—are you hurt?" A moment later, as she saw his hands were free and that he was uninjured, she would have given anything to recall her words. She had a wild hope that perhaps, concerned in looking at the damage to the window, he had not heard them.

But he had! He swung round, facing her with amazement in his eyes: amazement — yes, and something else, something she could not read.

"*What* did you say?"

"I only asked—I was afraid that you were hurt . . ."

"You called me darling. *And what's more, you meant it!*"

Her hands flew up to hide her crimsoning face. "No— oh, no! It must have been the shock — I don't know why I——"

"I do! Because you love me. As I love you."

He took her unresisting in his arms, and bent his head to silence further argument with his mouth . . . She learned now that it could be passionate as well as resolute, ardent as well as ruthless. She felt as though his strength flowed through her in a vital current, and the steady beating of his heart beneath her cheek became the rhythm of the universe, while the passing minutes added into an eternity of understanding, needing no words to express it.

Barclay raised his head at last, and murmured, with his cheek against her hair, the question every lover asks sooner or later. "Darling, how long is it since you knew . . .?"

"Since I knew I loved you? With me, it all began that evening when you asked me to have dinner with you . . ."

"So that we could thrash out what best to do about the gossip over your being here? That time?"

"Yes . . . Until then, I had detested you! I'd thought you arrogant and domineering and thoroughly exasperating! And then, when we had talked it over and agreed to take no notice, we went on to talk of other things—your work, and so on—I began to realize that—well, that my ideas about you had been all wrong. And from that time on, every single thought has led to you." She sighed, remembering the time of loneliness and longing: sighed again, for happiness.

"But why, if that was how it was, did you refuse to marry me?"

She drew away from him a little, laying her hands against his chest, while Barclay's hands behind her back still held her lightly clasped. Their eyes looked into one another's as Verity protested, "How *could* I say I'd marry you, when you made no pretence of wanting me for any other reason than to solve your problem about Julia's future? No hint of anything involved except material benefits for both of us! Not a single word of love! . . . I would have done it, all the same, hoping that — well that sharing life together might eventually deepen what you felt for me until you loved me as — as I loved you. But I was afraid it mightn't work out that way — that being tied to me, not loving me, might prove to be an irritation, and ultimately make you love me less, instead of more."

"My dearest heart, I loved you so intolerably that it was sheer hell to offer marriage to you as a sort of business proposition."

"But why, *why* did you?"

"I'd meant to wait a bit. Then circumstances forced my hand. But still I felt I must go warily, and give you all the time you needed."

She was bewildered. "Time for what?"

"For readjustment. I knew — my mother told me — of the unhappiness and disillusion you had gone through before you came here. I gathered that it might be quite a while before you could get over your distrust and fear of —well, of men, and love, and life in general."

She gave a little shaken laugh. "*You* cured me of all that—oh, weeks and months ago! Now tell me something else. Why did you fall in so readily with Dr. Gairloch's advice, and make arrangements to send Julia and me away tomorrow, without a word of ever coming back?"

He laughed. "Janice had nothing whatever to do with that decision, though she liked to think she had! Even before Julia was ill I had been contemplating something of the sort, thinking that it mightn't be a bad idea for you to leave here for a time unspecified: hoping that when you were away from me, perhaps you'd realize that—well, that 'Absence makes the heart grow fonder' might be true."

It was her turn to laugh. "And all the time, if you had only known . . .! Darling, you've got to get this straight, once and for all. I fell in love with love. Never with Euan. Never with anyone but you!"

The sound of voices, followed by approaching footsteps, made them draw apart. An instant later the door opened to admit Margaret Duncan. With a hostile glance at Verity she turned to Barclay. "Janice has come up. When you're finished giving Miss Cator her instructions, she wants to ask you what you think about some letter she has had."

"Tell her," said Barclay, "that I haven't time. She'd better consult someone else. Verity has at long last agreed to marry me, and we shall be busy all the evening making plans."

The look of horrified dismay upon Miss Duncan's face, the thought of the reactions in the drawing-room when she broke the news to Janice Gairloch, would have more than compensated Verity for their behaviour — had she wanted compensation. But the radiance of the present, and the promise of the future, had obliterated all the troubles, all the shadows of the past.

Hours later, Verity began to wonder whether sleep would ever come to her tonight — not that sleeplessness was any hardship, with her memories of the evening for company, and the unbelievable, ecstatic knowledge that before the month was out she would be Barclay's wife. *His wife . . . !*

A fortnight hence he was to come to Southwold, bringing with him Mary Pridham to take charge of Julia, who loved her dearly, for the next few weeks. Verity would return with him to London on the following day. Meanwhile he would have made arrangements for their wedding to take place immediately, and after, they would go to Scotland for their honeymoon . . . She wondered whether he were lying wakeful, too . . .

Restless, presently she rose, and sat herself upon the window seat. The chilly wind, which in the morning had been blowing from the east, had dropped. A southerly breeze, balmy and mild, caressed her gently as she sat there looking out. It bore no trace of petrol, now the streets were empty, but odors of moist earth, and budding trees in London's parks and squares. High overhead, the voices of migratory birds bound for their immemorial nesting places in the north cried to one another faintly. In the light of a street lamp she saw that in a window box belonging to the house opposite, a daffodil bud was bursting from its sheath.

Spring, after all, had come to Harley Street!

THE END

Harlequin Presents..

EACH MONTH —
FOUR GREAT NOVELS

~~~~~~

Here are the Latest Titles:

~~~~~~

ALL BOOKS 75c
On sale at your local retail store now.

Harlequin Romances

A JAMBOREE OF GREAT RE-ISSUES !

ALL BOOKS 60c

These titles are available at your local bookseller, or through the Harlequin Reader Service, M.P.O. Box 707, Niagara Falls, N.Y. 14302; Canadian address 649 Ontario St., Stratford, Ont.

UU